"I can't remember my name...or why I'm here."

"Do you remember riffin asked. He could see his car ahead of them and still no sign of the men who'd been after her.

"Two," she said.

"Are you sure?"

She nodded.

He unlocked his car, then headed toward the motorcycles. "Go get inside. You'll be safe."

"Where are you going?"

"I'll be right back. I promise."

Sunlight broke through the gray clouds above them as he quickly searched the tree line for the men. For the moment, his number one priority had to be getting her to safety. The problem was he still had no idea where the men were. And that had him worried. Not only were they armed, but he'd be outnumbered if they showed up.

He approached the motorcycles, quickly jerking out the spark plug wires on each bike.

But he was running out of time.

A bullet hit the side of his squad car.

Griffin ran back to his car and jerked open the driver's side door as the second bullet hit its mark...

Lisa Harris is a Christy Award winner and winner of the Best Inspirational Suspense Novel for 2011 from *RT Book Reviews*. She and her family are missionaries in southern Africa. When she's not working, she loves hanging out with her family, cooking different ethnic dishes, photography and heading into the African bush on safari. For more information about her books and life in Africa, visit her website at lisaharriswrites.com.

Books by Lisa Harris

Love Inspired Suspense

Final Deposit
Stolen Identity
Deadly Safari
Taken
Desperate Escape
Desert Secrets
Fatal Cover-Up
Deadly Exchange
No Place to Hide
Sheltered by the Soldier
Christmas Witness Pursuit

Visit the Author Profile page at Harlequin.com.

CHRISTMAS WITNESS PURSUIT

LISA HARRIS

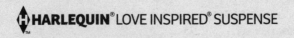

Recycling programs for this product may not exist in your area.

LOVE INSPIRED BOOKS

ISBN-13: 978-1-335-23252-6

Christmas Witness Pursuit

Copyright © 2019 by Lisa Harris

All rights reserved. Except for use in any review, the reproduction or utilization of this work in whole or in part in any form by any electronic, mechanical or other means, now known or hereafter invented, including xerography, photocopying and recording, or in any information storage or retrieval system, is forbidden without the written permission of the editorial office, Love Inspired Books, 195 Broadway, New York, NY 10007 U.S.A.

This is a work of fiction. Names, characters, places and incidents are either the product of the author's imagination or are used fictitiously, and any resemblance to actual persons, living or dead, business establishments, events or locales is entirely coincidental.

This edition published by arrangement with Love Inspired Books.

® and TM are trademarks of Love Inspired Books, used under license. Trademarks indicated with ® are registered in the United States Patent and Trademark Office, the Canadian Intellectual Property Office and in other countries.

www.Harlequin.com

Printed in U.S.A.

And ye shall know the truth,
and the truth shall make you free.
–John 8:32

To those who long for freedom and comfort.
May you find healing in His presence.

ONE

The crack of gunfire ripped her out of the darkness. Ears ringing, she opened her eyes then had to wait for her blurred vision to clear. Everything around her spun while a thick dust filled her lungs with each breath.

She searched her surroundings through the haze. She was lying in the back seat of an unfamiliar car. Gray leather seats. A small duffel bag and red scarf beside her. Her gaze shifted to the front passenger seat, where a man slumped behind a deflated airbag, his head tilted at an odd angle while blood seeped through his suit jacket. The window beside him had shattered, leaving shards of glass covering the inside of the car and his body. A wave of confusion engulfed her. They'd clearly been in an accident, but no memories surfaced. Only panic.

Why couldn't she remember?

She sat up and pressed her hands against her head, trying to block out the pain pulsing through her temples. Pieces of memories fought to rise to the surface, but it was like a puzzle where she couldn't quite find the right pieces to snap into place. Couldn't find the answers she should know. Like, what was she doing there? Who was the man in the front seat? She glanced up and caught her dazed reflection in the rearview mirror. And who was she?

The man let out a low groan, turned and tried to grab for her hand. "You need to get out of here. They… they're after you."

She sucked in a sharp breath as she pulled away from him, not understanding. "Who?"

"Just…run."

His garbled words were clear enough for her to understand the stark warning. Still, she couldn't just leave him.

Could she?

She reached for his wrist, checked his weakened pulse then saw the FBI badge hanging around his neck.

"They're coming," he warned again. "Go. Now…"

Shouts escalated outside the vehicle. Another shot ripped through the air. She turned to see a second man dressed in a suit drop to the ground. She froze. Blood pooled onto the pavement beneath the body. She shifted her gaze beyond the downed man to two men, wearing black, running toward the car.

They're after you.

Go. Now…

There was no more time to think. She undid her seat belt, scrambled toward the door and shoved it open. The car had swerved off the side of the road, so the forested tree line beyond her was now only a few yards away. She had no weapons. No way to defend herself against the men. Her only possible protection, from what she could see, was the trees. She might not remember any details of why she was there, but she knew that the dying man in the front seat was right and the men coming for her had no intention to help her.

She jumped out of the car and fled into the forest. Her lungs felt as if they were going to explode from the cold air, but she had to keep moving. Her boots crunched through the underbrush. There was no real trail, just trees with thick brush beneath them as far as she could see, which meant leaving an untraceable path was going to be impossible.

Just like outrunning whoever was after her was probably going to be impossible.

Shoving the thought aside, she dodged a fallen branch, barely managing to keep her balance as she ducked beneath it. Her head felt as if someone was driving a stake through her temple, but she couldn't stop running. Not when she could hear the cracking of dry brush behind her as the men pursued her.

She glanced up at the gray sky above her, barely visible through the canopy of branches. She had no idea which direction she was running, but knew she needed to get as much distance between them as she could. If she found a way to lose them, she could head back to the road and flag down a passing car. At this point, she didn't care where she went. As long as she got as far away from the men as possible.

Fifty yards later she stumbled again over a dead log and tried to catch her balance, but this time she fell facedown onto the hard ground. Blood ran from a scratch on the palm of her hand, but she didn't even feel the sting. Instead she could hear them behind her, crashing through the brush as they got closer. It would be only a matter of seconds before they found her. There was a thick layer of brush ahead to her right. It would provide her with cover. If she could hide there…

Still on the ground, she crawled through the brush, praying it was thick enough to camouflage her, then lay flat and still against the cold ground. Seconds later her pursuers hurried past, not even half a dozen feet from her hiding place. Her fingers were numb and her lungs burned with each breath as she waited for them to vanish into the forest.

She let out a silent sigh of relief when the men didn't stop. She'd wait for them to get out of sight then head back toward the road. Unless… She swallowed hard as one of the men stopped suddenly, held up his hand and turned around, suspending her plan. The wind howled above her through the trees. She pressed her body into the slight indention where she lay, willing her heart to slow down.

Keep me hidden from these men, God…

The prayer came instinctively, without hesitation.

"What's wrong?" the second man stopped and looked back.

The first headed toward where she lay. "I can't hear her anymore."

"She can't be that far ahead. We need to keep going."

"Just wait a minute." The first man turned in a slow circle, close enough she could make out the biker patch on his leather jacket. Close enough she was certain he could hear her heart pounding inside her chest.

Panic mushroomed inside her. If they found her now…

"We're wasting time. Let's go."

The first man continued to study the terrain a few more moments before finally nodding his head.

She waited until they disappeared into the brush and then slowly counted to twenty before coming out of her hiding place and running in the opposite direction. She might not remember what had happened or even who she was, but one thing was clear. If they found her, they would kill her.

Deputy Griffin O'Callaghan called in the single-vehicle accident and asked for backup and an emergency crew as he approached the wreck south of Timber Falls. A car had spun off the road and landed in the ditch. Two motorcycles sat behind the vehicle, but from a quick observation, neither looked as if it had been involved in the accident. He stepped out onto the road, his boots crunching against the gravel as he walked toward the wrecked vehicle then paused.

A man in a suit lay on the side of the road, shot in the temple. Griffin checked for a pulse then noticed the man's gun and FBI badge. A second victim lay slumped over in the front passenger seat, once again shot. This was no accident scene. These men had been executed. But where were the drivers of the motorcycles?

There was a small bag next to a woman's red winter scarf in the back seat and the side door was open. He worked to put the pieces together. Whoever had been in the back was, more than likely, either a prisoner being transported or a witness being protected.

He grabbed a file off the front floorboard and quickly scanned the contents. There were no names, just instructions on the transportation of a witness to Denver and a court case number. He folded the papers and shoved them in his back pocket as he took a step away from the car and noticed the bullet casings scattered on the scene. There were bullet holes in the front passenger door, one of the tires had been shot out and a window was shattered.

A disturbing picture began to play out in his mind. The men on the motorcycles had shot the agent in the front seat either during or after the crash. The second agent had then taken a bullet trying to protect the witness in an apparent shoot-out. The witness had run, but the two hit men had gone after her.

Griffin moved away from the car toward the tree line, where he quickly found three sets of footprints leading into the forest. The witness was probably going to end up running in circles then being shot by the men after her. Or getting lost and freezing to death in the storm that was about to hit this part of the country. Neither scenario was acceptable because, either way, she'd be dead.

Like Lilly.

His stomach clenched at the unwanted memories that rushed to the surface. He shoved them aside, forcing himself to focus on the situation at hand. This was not the time to dredge up the past. Instead he updated the sheriff's office on his status as he headed into the woods after her. He moved quickly but purposefully, studying the ground until the three sets of tracks he'd been following stopped and seemed to converge around one spot.

Griffin paused again. Something had happened here. His father had always taught him that tracking was like learning to read, a challenge that had always fascinated him. They'd spent hours out on the ranch training to interpret the terrain as they identified animals, studied the surroundings and traced their travel routes. Today he was praying his skills would help him save a woman's life.

He squatted down, ignoring the blistering cold. Two people had continued south after stopping. A third had doubled back before taking a new path toward the main road. It had to be the witness.

Griffin found her heading for the main road about a hundred yards south of the wreck. There was still no sign of the motorcyclists, but he knew he couldn't let his guard down. He had no doubt they were still out there. He held up his badge as he ran to catch up with her. Shouting at her to stop wasn't an option. It would only lead whoever was out there straight to her. But losing her wasn't an option, either. He chased her another ten feet then hurried to stop in front of her.

He held up his hands so she could see his badge. "Ma'am…don't scream. Please. I'm a sheriff's deputy and I can keep you safe."

She stumbled backward. He'd seen the accident aftermath and knew she had to be terrified. And, with her escorts dead, she probably had no idea who she could trust. He needed that person to be him.

"I know someone's trying to find you," he rushed on to say. "I'm here to help."

She hesitated then nodded. "They killed those men."

"I know. We're going to head to my car," he said, "then I'll take you directly to the sheriff's office in Timber Falls."

"They were FBI?" she asked as they started walking.

"Yes." He placed his hand on her arm, wondering why she didn't already know the answer to her question. "Do you know who killed them?"

"I'm guessing the same people who are after me, but I have no idea who they are."

"You're okay now. I'm going to get you somewhere safe." He picked up the pace slightly, his senses on high alert, knowing it was just a matter of time before her hunters realized she'd doubled back to the road. Letting them find her wasn't an option. "What's your name?"

She hesitated then shook her head. "I don't know."

He stopped for a moment, confused. "Wait... You don't remember your name?"

She glanced up at him with those big brown eyes and long lashes of hers, giving him a brief moment to study her while he waited for her to answer. Five-foot-five, maybe six, dark hair past her shoulders... She had a lost look in her eyes that pulled at that familiar spot in his heart, making him want to protect her all the more. Her only visible injuries were a scrape on her hand and a bruise forming at her temple. But maybe he was missing something.

She shook her head. "I know it sounds crazy, but I can't remember."

"What about today's date?"

"It's... I don't know. What is it?"

"December tenth." He'd caught the panic in her voice as she struggled to answer. "What can you remember?"

Her eyes avoided the scene in front of them. "Nothing before the accident. The man in the front seat had been shot. He told me to run. That they were coming after me."

"Okay…" Griffin wasn't sure if her loss of memory was a sign of something more serious but, for now, he just needed to get her out of there alive. "Don't worry about that right now. Do you hurt anywhere?" he asked.

"My head, but that's all. That and, of course, the fact that I can't remember my name or why I'm here."

"Do you remember how many were chasing you?" he asked as they finally emerged onto the main road. He could see his car ahead of them and still no sign of the men who'd been after her.

"Two," she said.

"Are you sure?"

She nodded.

Her answer surprised him. There were three helmets on the bikes. She could be wrong, though it seemed to be the events after the crash that she could remember—like the dead bodies at the scene and the men chasing after her—but not events or things that had happened before the accident, including her name. Either she'd hit her head or was experiencing some kind of dissociative amnesia from the trauma. But the whys didn't matter right now.

He clicked the key fob as they approached his vehicle and unlocked his car, then headed toward the motorcycles. "Go get inside. You'll be safe."

"Where are you going?"

"I'll be right back. I promise."

Sunlight broke through the gray clouds above them as he quickly searched the tree line for the men. If he hadn't had to worry about the woman, he would have gone after them. However, for the moment, his number-one priority had to be to get her to safety. The problem was that he still had no idea where the men were. And that had him worried. Not only were they armed, he'd be outnumbered if they showed up. That meant ensuring she wasn't hit in any cross fire would be difficult, so he had to slow the men down. He stopped next to the two motorcycles and quickly jerked out the spark plug wires on each bike.

But he was running out of time. He could now hear the men crashing through the underbrush without even bothering to quiet their steps. A bullet hit the side of his squad car. He ran back to his car and jerked open the driver's-side door. A searing pain shot through him as the second bullet hit its mark.

TWO

She couldn't breathe and her heart felt as if it were about to burst out of her chest. She'd just been rescued from the men trying to kill her, but this was far from over. Blood was rapidly spreading across the deputy's right sleeve as he spoke to his dispatcher to give an update on the situation.

"You've been hit," she said as he disconnected the call.

"It's just a flesh wound. My primary goal right now is to get you out of here. Backup is on its way to arrest the guys that attacked you."

She stared out the rear window to where the men were trying to figure out why their bikes wouldn't start and then focused back on his arm. "You have no idea how bad it is. You're running on adrenaline now. I need to look at it, and you certainly shouldn't be driving."

"We're twenty minutes out of Timber Falls," he said, pressing on the accelerator. "I can wait that long to get treated."

"We need to get the bleeding stopped before then." She grabbed for a T-shirt on the back seat and started pressing it against the wound. This was insane. She couldn't remember her name or what she did for a living, but somehow her response felt automatic. "What kind of first-aid equipment do you have in the back of your car?"

"A basic medical kit, exam gloves, a tourniquet..."

She pressed the shirt tighter, praying the bleeding stopped. "What did you do to their bikes?"

"They're disabled for now."

"So they can't follow us?"

"Not unless they flag down a ride. I've got their spark plug wires."

"That will buy us some time." But she needed to stop the bleeding now. "I might not know my name, but somehow I know how to deal with this. Are you feeling light-headed?"

"No."

"Nauseated?"

"No."

She felt for his pulse. It was fast but strong and steady. "I should drive."

"Except you've just been in involved in an accident and hit your head. Out of the two of us, I'm definitely in a better position to get us out of here."

"We make quite a pair." She frowned at his stubbornness, but wasn't backing down. "Drive another three or four miles then pull over so I can patch you up properly."

"I'm not sure we should stop—"

"A gunshot wound isn't something to play around with, and you're losing blood. I need to assess how serious it is."

She took his nod as confirmation that he would do

what she asked, then listened as he spent the next mile or two telling her what he'd found out at the scene. The FBI badges and the file that said they'd been transporting a witness for a trial…

"Do you remember any of this?" he asked.

She fought to resurrect memories she knew had to be there, but instead only encountered a mounting frustration. "I'm sorry, but no. I can't remember anything."

"Don't worry about it. Your memories will return."

"Maybe, but from what you're telling me, I'm not sure I want to remember."

What had she seen? It had to have been something horrible, like another murder.

A minute later he pulled the car off at an overlook with a stunning view of the mountains to the west. But she barely saw it. Instead her mind was fighting to focus on the one thing she knew she could do. She hurried to the trunk of the car with him then started going through his first-aid kit, trying not to give in to the panic.

Seconds later she carefully helped him out of his jacket and uniform, leaving on his T-shirt, so she could get to the wound.

"Ouch."

Her eyes widened. "Don't tell me you're one of those macho men who faint at the sight of blood."

"Hardly, but you've got to give me a little credit. I was just shot."

"According to you, it's just an insignificant flesh wound."

"Are you always this ornery?" He shot her a stern look, but his eyes were smiling.

Do you flirt with every woman you have contact with?

She bit back the question on the tip of her tongue.

"Honestly, I have no idea." She shrugged, unable to avoid his grin or to ignore just how good-looking he was with those dark brown eyes. She shoved the ridiculous thoughts away.

"The good news is that you were right about one thing," she said. "The bullet skimmed your arm and the blood's already clotting. You'll need stiches, but you'll survive."

He smiled again. "That's a relief."

She looked way, focusing on his arm as she disinfected her hands then started cleaning the wound. The routine seemed familiar. Comfortable. And was the first time she'd felt in control since the accident.

Or at least as much as I can feel in control in a situation like this.

The reminder sent panic flooding through her again. She might not remember why she'd been in that car, but she did know those men were still out there. And something told her that missing spark plug wires weren't going to slow them down for long.

She opened a butterfly bandage to hold the wound together, trying to stomp out her anxiety at the same time. "They could have flagged down a car to follow us."

"I know. But there aren't a lot of cars out on these back roads right now, especially with the storm coming. Besides, backup should be there by now."

"I hope so."

"Which means we're even now," he said. "I saved your life and now you've saved mine."

She shook her head. "Your life hardly needed saving. Anyone could do this, though it seems…familiar."

A memory flashed to the forefront. She was running

through a long hall with tiled white floors. Someone was calling a name.

Tory.

Her name.

His hand on her shoulder brought her back to the present. "You okay?"

She nodded, her hands shaking as she repacked the first-aid kit. "I remembered something. My name's Tory."

He pulled his shirt back on and started buttoning it up. "That's wonderful. And it means your memory's coming back."

"Slowly, but I still feel like I'm fighting my way through this heavy fog."

He smiled at her. "It's nice to meet you, Tory. I'm Griffin, by the way."

"It's nice to meet you, as well." His smile managed to erase some of her tension. "So we now know three things. My name's Tory. I'm a witness in a case. And someone wants me dead."

"Well, when you put it that way, it doesn't sound quite so wonderful."

"I guess there isn't a nice way to put that, is there?" She laughed. "I'm just finding it kind of ironic that someone's after me for what I know, but I can't remember what it is."

"Don't worry." He slammed the trunk shut then headed for the driver's seat. "We're going to figure this out, Tory... But for now, we need to get out of here."

She climbed back into the front passenger seat, knowing he was right. She needed to find a way to fight the panic and stay focused on the fact that at least they were both alive.

Unlike the FBI agents.

"How are you feeling?" Griffin flipped on his blinker then sped back onto the highway.

"Seems like I'm the one who should be asking you that question."

"Oh, you don't have to worry about me. I happen to have a really good doctor. In fact, she told me I'm going to live."

Tory tucked a strand of hair behind her ear. "Are you always this funny?"

"My brothers would probably say no. That I'm the serious one of the bunch. But you didn't answer my question."

She smiled again, wondering how he kept doing that. Distracting her from the situation. "I'm okay for now. I just wish I could remember something significant."

"Remembering your name's pretty significant. That, and I think we might have figured out your profession."

She leaned back against the seat. "Somewhere I must have picked up some medical experience."

"I'm thinking a paramedic or maybe an ER doctor."

"Maybe, but I'd suggest we don't test that theory."

He couldn't help but chuckle. "I have to agree with you on that one."

Even his smile couldn't put her totally at ease. Two men had just died protecting her. She could not let that happen again.

Griffin glanced out his rearview mirror as he sped toward town, glad they'd finally made it onto the main highway.

More often than not, women made him feel nervous.

As much as he enjoyed the small talk with the woman sitting next to him, he couldn't shake the worry that whoever was after her was going to find her. On top of that, his arm felt as if it were on fire. But he couldn't worry about that now. He was more concerned that the men who'd killed the FBI agents would find a way to pick up his tail despite his attempt to disable their motorcycles.

He was convinced they weren't dealing with amateurs. The attack against the FBI escort had clearly been strategic. The drivers had known the route and had planned their assault. But at least Tory was safe for the moment. If she hadn't escaped into the woods when she had, they'd either have her or she'd be dead now.

The other pressing concern was the weather. The news had been reporting for days that a huge storm system was sweeping in from the north. That meant he was going to need to get her somewhere safe before the roads became too dangerous to use.

Tory pressed her hands together in her lap then stared out the window. "It's starting to snow again. How far out of Timber Falls are we?"

"Just a couple minutes."

"Good. And it looks like the bleeding from your arm has stopped."

His phone rang and he glanced at the caller ID. It was the sheriff's office. He hoped they were calling with an update.

"What's your ETA?" Sheriff Jackson asked as soon as Griffin answered.

"We're almost to the Timber Falls exit."

"Good. Just to be on the safe side, I've arranged for Dr. Swanson to meet you at the back entrance of the clinic. You should be able to slip the witness in without being noticed. Someone will also be there to sew you up if needed."

"Thank you, but please tell me you found the guys who did this?"

"I wish I could say we did, but when backup arrived at the scene, they found the bikes, but no signs of the men. I put out a BOLO from the descriptions you gave us, but it's not going to be easy to search for them with this storm coming in."

"What about the accident scene?" Griffin took the exit and headed straight to the clinic located on the edge of the small town. "Was anything found that might give us answers?"

"That's going to take time. The coroner just arrived to pick up the bodies. They've been ID'd as special agents Lincoln and Adler...but that's really all we know at this point."

Griffin frowned. He needed some good news. "Have you heard from the FBI yet?"

"I'm still waiting for them to call back. I'll let you know as soon as they do."

Frustrated, Griffin hung up then drove through the back of the clinic parking lot. "I know this has got to be unsettling."

Her lower lip trembled. "I can't get their faces out of my mind. They died trying to protect me."

He parked in an empty space near the back door and shut off the engine, fighting the urge to pull her into his arms to tell her everything was going to be okay. Because he knew the truth. Sometimes things didn't turn out the way you wanted. Sometimes, no matter how hard he tried, everything wouldn't be okay.

"You know none of this is your fault," he said finally.

"Really? Because the way I see it, those agents were killed because of me." She stared straight ahead, that lost look back in her eyes. "It just seems so crazy. All the things I want to remember I can't, and yet no matter how hard I try, I can't get the picture out of my mind of that agent being shot and dying in front of me."

"I'm so sorry you saw what you did. Sorry your being in the wrong place at the wrong time put you in this situation in the first place."

"I guess as a deputy you would understand death." She turned and caught his gaze. "Does it ever fade, some of the things you see?"

He looked away, wanting to ignore her question, but knew he couldn't. "I've had to learn to deal with things I've seen, but that still doesn't always make it easy. There are faces and stories I'll never be able to forget."

"Thank you for what you've done for me."

He shrugged off the gratitude, ready for a change in subject. "I'm just doing my job."

"Maybe, but you saved my life."

Thirty minutes later the nurse had just finished stitching up Griffin's arm when his phone rang again. He stepped into the small hallway at the back of the clinic for privacy and took the call.

"Deputy O'Callaghan…this is FBI Special Agent Mark Hill. I understand you have one of our witnesses in your custody. Victoria Faraday."

"I do. We're at the clinic in Timber Falls and she's in with the doctor right now."

"The report I received said she's suffering from memory loss and you'd been shot."

"I'm waiting for a report from the doctor about her, but yes. Thankfully the bullet just grazed me." Griffin took a deep breath before asking, "I'm assuming you've received the news that both your agents were killed?"

"Unfortunately, yes."

Griffin hesitated. "I'm extremely sorry for your loss."

"So am I. They were good men that are going to be greatly missed. Jinx Ryder—the man behind this—has been a thorn in the FBI's side for far too long."

"What can you tell me about the case?"

"I can send you the file…but, briefly, she was out hiking eight months ago and witnessed the brutal murder of a couple not too far from where you are."

"I remember that headline."

"We'd been hunting Jinx for over a year. He's suspected to be involved in a dozen other felonies, but we've never been able to pin anything on the man. Not until Victoria Faraday."

"And she's your eye witness."

"Our only witness. That is why I need your help. The highway north of you was just shut down, which means it's going to take some time to get anyone to you. They're calling this the storm of the decade."

Griffin glanced at the closed door where Tory was still meeting with the doctor. "What do you need me to do?"

"She's going to need protection until we can get there."

Griffin frowned. Playing the role of bodyguard wasn't exactly on his to-do list for the weekend. While he wasn't keen on babysitting, neither was he willing to leave her stranded.

"Can you get her somewhere safe for the next forty-eight hours or at least until this storm passes? Somewhere out of the way and secure until I can get someone there?"

Griffin mentally flipped through his limited options. "My parents own a ranch not far from here. I suppose I could take her there for a couple of days. It's unlikely these guys would be able to track her down."

"Sounds like the perfect plan. And, Deputy O'Callaghan…this needs to stay under the radar. Jinx clearly has a long arm. Someone was able to track down that escort—"

"Exactly, which has me worried." Griffin vacillated, but he needed to know what was going on. "If you want to ensure her safety, you need to find out where your leak is."

"I can assure you there is no leak—"

"I'm sorry, Agent Hill, but two of your agents were just murdered and your witness barely escaped with her life."

"And we are doing everything we can to find out how that happened."

At the end of the hall, Tory stepped out of the examination room with the doctor.

"I need to go," the FBI agent said, "but keep me updated."

Griffin frowned as he hung up. If the FBI didn't find their leak—or at least admit they had one—keeping Tory safe might prove impossible.

THREE

Tory stepped into the clinic hallway with the doctor, wishing he had given her a prescription to restore her memory. Instead he'd told her all she could really do was watch for symptoms and wait for her memories to return. But that was easier said than done. She was tired of fighting to resurrect memories she knew were there but couldn't find. And scared at how vulnerable that made her feel.

"Deputy O'Callaghan…" The doctor dropped his pen into his front jacket pocket as Griffin walked up to them. "Sorry we took so long, but I wanted to make sure I didn't miss anything."

"That's fine," Griffin said then turned to her. "How are you feeling?"

"While I did hit my head in the accident, the doctor believes my amnesia should resolve itself eventually."

"That sounds like good news."

"It is," Dr. Swanson said. "In the meantime, she'll feel as if her thoughts and memories are clouded, but clearly they are already slowly returning, which is a

good sign. I would, though, like to keep her here overnight for observation—"

"I'm not sure that's a good idea." Griffin shook his
head. "Staying here would make it harder to limit who
knows where she is. And the more people who know,
the riskier this whole situation becomes."

Tory felt another wave of panic hit. "Then what am
I supposed to do? Is the FBI sending someone else?"

"Because of the storm, they won't be able to get any
agents here for at least forty-eight hours. They've asked
me to ensure your safety until they get here."

She worked to process the news. If trained FBI agents
hadn't been able to stop an attack, how was Griffin—
a local sheriff's deputy—supposed to keep her safe?
She'd never be able to live with someone else dying
trying to protect her.

"This isn't your case—"

"No," he said, "but I do have a solution. I want to
take you to my family ranch, which is about thirty minutes from town. If we leave now, we should get there
before the storm hits."

She pressed her fingertips against her temples, trying
to deal with the fact that once again she was having to
trust her life to a stranger. "I don't know—"

"It's just a precaution until the storm passes. You'll
be safe there."

"Will I?" She looked up at him, unconvinced. "Two
agents are dead, which means I'd be putting your family
at risk. And who's to say they can't find me there, too?"

She didn't want to sound ungrateful, because she
wasn't. But she barely knew this man, and now he
wanted to take her to his home to keep her safe? There

had to be another option. Surely the roads weren't that bad yet. If they could get to Denver, there had to be an FBI safe house where she could stay until this nightmare was over. Something that wouldn't involve him and his family.

"I know this all has to be overwhelming," Griffin said, "but my job now is to keep you safe. Plus, my mom's a nurse and she'll be able to keep an eye on any medical issues." He turned back to the doctor. "I'm trusting you to keep this situation confidential."

"You know I will and, with Tory's permission," the doctor said, "I can give your mother a call and update her, so she knows exactly what she needs to watch for."

Tory knew Griffin must have read the doubt in her eyes, along with the fear she couldn't shake. She might not remember what she'd eaten for breakfast yesterday, but she knew she hated feeling out of control. And that was exactly how she felt right now. But what choice did she have? Someone wanted her dead and she certainly wasn't in a position to handle this on her own.

"I need you to trust me," Griffin said.

She shot him a weak smile. "You did save my life once."

"And I'm going to do everything I can to make sure you stay safe, but we need to leave now. Once the storm hits, I don't want to be out on these roads." Griffin caught her gaze, reminding her how she'd become totally dependent on the deputy. "Are you okay with the plan?"

She nodded, despite the fact she wasn't convinced they were doing the right thing. What if those men tried to come after her again? Deputy O'Callaghan might have saved her once, but she'd seen what those men could do, and he was only one man.

She glanced down the hallway at the six-foot-tall Christmas tree made from blown-up surgical gloves and an IV pole and loneliness surged through her. It was Christmastime and she couldn't even remember who was waiting for her back home to celebrate the holidays. Surely there were family, friends and maybe even someone special in her life. Why couldn't she remember?

Griffin hesitated in front of her. "Are you sure you're okay?"

She forced a smile. "I will be."

Because she didn't have a choice.

"I just need to stop by the sheriff's office," Griffin said. "Then we'll head out of town."

Twenty minutes later they were driving toward the O'Callaghan ranch that was nestled beneath impressive views of Pikes Peak and the surrounding mountains while the sun slipped toward the horizon in front of them. On any other day, she would be soaking up the beauty of the wintery terrain. Right now, all she wanted to do was to run far away from everything that had happened.

"What are your parents going to say when you bring home a complete stranger?" she asked, breaking the silence between them.

"Trust me, my family won't think twice about it. It's definitely not the first time one of us has brought home someone needing a place to stay."

She couldn't help but smile. "You make me sound like a stray cat."

He chuckled. "We've taken in a few of those over the years, as well."

"Funny. Tell me about your family. You said earlier you had brothers." She needed a distraction. Something to stop her from worrying about what could happen and the memories that still refused to surface.

"For starters, I've got three brothers."

"Wow…your mother had her hands full."

"More than you could ever imagine, but thankfully for her we're all grown up now. Caden works with my father on the ranch and is a former army ranger. Reid works for the local fire department and my youngest brother, Liam, is in the army and recently got married."

"He's the only one with a wife?"

"Yep. They have a sweet daughter, Mia."

His response surprised her. If his brothers were even close to being as good-looking as Griffin, the three of them sounded like catches. She glanced at her own ringless left hand. She was going to assume she wasn't married or engaged but, for all she knew, she had a boyfriend back home.

Wherever that was.

She cleared her throat. "So, three bachelors. How did that happen?"

"That's a question my mom asks almost every time I see her."

"What about your ranch?" she asked, changing the subject. "Sounds like a wonderful place to grow up."

"It was. Our family has worked the land since the 1920s. It's got over ten thousand acres and some of the best hunting in the area, and is still used for hay production, livestock grazing and raising cattle."

"Sounds beautiful, too." Nevertheless, there was still the lingering question she couldn't shake. "What if something goes wrong? What if they find me and it puts your family in danger? I couldn't do that—"

"We'll deal with that when—and if—the time comes. But don't worry about that now."

"Okay, then that must mean it's time for you to ask me about my family, except I don't have any answers."

"Have you remembered anything new?"

"Nothing more than a handful of fuzzy memories."

"We know your name and that you have medical training. I suppose we can always Google you." Griffin glanced toward the back seat. "The FBI sent over a brief file on the case. That's what I picked up at the sheriff's office. There's supposed to be something on you, as well."

"Really?" She grabbed the folder, suddenly nervous about what she was going to find out.

The file was thin and the documents had been redacted in several places, including her hometown, but reading through it felt more like reading someone else's biography.

"Does anything stand out or jog your memory?" Griffin asked.

"Not really, but there's not much. It says parents are dead, and no siblings." She looked up at him. "I'm going to assume I have a friend or two."

"I'd say you definitely have way more than just a friend or two."

"And why would you say that? I could be some recluse who lives with a houseful of cats and only goes out to check the mail."

"Somehow I don't think so. You're easy to talk to,

you have a sense of humor, and we already know how well you do in a medical emergency."

She couldn't help but smile. She liked the way he managed to disarm her fears and make her laugh. "Keep trying to make me feel better. You're doing a good job."

"There's something else," he said. "I know you put your life on the line to put a murderer behind bars. Something like that takes a lot of courage."

His statement brought on another flash of memory, but she could not quite grab on to it. She glanced out the window at the falling snow that had already left a dusting of white across the landscape. She might have had to risk her life for justice, but even if that were true, it did little to erase the terror that wouldn't leave her alone.

Griffin studied her reaction for a moment as they headed down the two-lane dirt road toward the ranch, knowing everything that had happened had left her unsettled. He couldn't blame her. Not only was her life in danger, she could not remember what had brought her to this point beyond what had been written in an FBI report.

"I meant what I said. What you did took a lot of courage."

"Maybe, but I'm just trying to figure all this out without getting too terrified. I keep asking myself the same question. What was my motivation? I obviously had to realize there was going to be a cost." She skimmed through the file. "There's a section in here about Jinx Ryder. He's been arrested for racketeering, conspiracy to launder money, murder, and is known to be involved in several criminal enterprises. Sounds to me like anyone would be crazy to cross this guy."

"Or extremely brave," he countered.

"I'm not feeling brave." Tory drummed her fingers against the armrest. "Instead I'm wondering what made me think I could survive going up against this guy."

He felt his jaw tighten as he debated whether or not to share with her what had been nagging him all afternoon. What he had to say would shake her already precarious world, something he didn't want to do. But if there was any chance that he was right...

"What are you thinking?" she asked, somehow sensing the shift in his thoughts.

"What if they weren't trying to kill you?" he asked, feeling the burn in his arm.

Her eyes widened as she glanced up at him. "I'm not sure I understand. They killed the men transporting me, chased me through the woods and then shot at the car as we left. I'd say they were definitely trying to kill me."

"They killed the agents you were with and shot at me. Did they ever shoot directly at you?"

His question seemed to throw her off. "They shot at the car."

"Yes, but what if they were trying to stop the FBI detail. To extract you. Alive."

"Alive?"

He hesitated again, knowing that what he was saying would probably make no sense from her point of view. From the little they'd been told about the case, it seemed clear that Jinx and his men's only objective was to silence her. She was the sole witness to a heinous crime, and it didn't matter if she could remember the details or not. She had the evidence the FBI needed to put Jinx behind bars for life.

"Why would they want to me alive?" she asked. "I'm a witness to a murder. Aren't I better off dead to them?"

"That's an obvious assumption, but there are things that don't add up."

"Like?"

Griffin searched for the words to clarify what he was thinking. "What if you have information they want? Something that would make you worth more to them alive than dead?"

"Like what? Because at this point even if that were true, I can't remember the murder, let alone any information I might have."

"True, but they don't know that. Just think about it. There were two men after you, but three helmets on the bikes. And on top of that, they never shot at you. They killed the agents and they were shooting at me."

"I'm not convinced you're right, but until I get my memory back, I have no way of knowing."

"I'm sorry." His parents' house appeared in the distance as the snow began to fall heavier. "I shouldn't have brought it up."

"What I do know is that they found me once and I'm sure they can find me again. I'm the only witness in a case that could put Jinx behind bars for the rest of his life. That's pretty strong motivation on his part to get rid of me."

He didn't miss the fear in her voice as she spoke, making him regret he'd ever brought it up. "Forget all of that for now. All we really need to do is to focus on keeping you safe."

"And when the storm passes?" she asked.

"We'll get you to Denver. But it won't be easy for them to trace you here."

"Are you sure? What's to stop them from finding me here just like they found my escort?"

"The sheriff's office is going to be on alert, and I'll also make sure our ranch hands are on the lookout for anything suspicious."

Beyond that, all he could do was pray it would be enough to keep her safe.

Griffin's phone rang, interrupting their conversation. He checked the caller ID and opted to answer on his cell instead of through the car's speaker system.

Thirty seconds later he ended the call. "That was the FBI."

"Why do I have the feeling this isn't going to be good news?"

"Because it isn't." His frown deepened. He wished he could find a way to lessen the blow. "Jinx was in the process of being transferred to a new facility, so he'd be near the courthouse for the trial."

"Griffin...what happened?"

He sucked in a sharp breath. "Jinx escaped."

FOUR

It didn't matter that she couldn't remember Jinx Ryder's face, or even all the details of what she'd witnessed. Tory knew enough about the situation to realize her life was in danger. Now that Jinx had managed to escape from custody, there was a good chance he'd come after her himself. And that terrified her.

"Would you like more bread?"

Tory jumped at the question clearly posed at her and looked up at the basket of garlic bread Griffin's mom, Marci, was holding. She wondered how long the older woman had been waiting for her to answer.

Tory grabbed a piece then passed the basket to Griffin. "I'm sorry."

"You have nothing to be sorry about." Marci's smile seemed genuine, just like everything else about his family. "This entire situation has to be unsettling for you."

"I just can't stop jumping at every shadow." She glanced across the room as if to prove her point, but the reaction was automatic. "I'm convinced he's going to come after me himself."

"Not any time soon." Griffin's dad, Jacob, looked up

from his bowl of stew. "I've lived in these mountains my whole life, and I'll be the first one to tell you that he'd be a fool to try to find you in this kind of weather. I know every inch of this ranch, and trust me, even I'm still planning on staying right here in this house until the weather clears."

Tory could hear the wind howling against the side of the house, giving her a tangible reminder of the storm now brewing outside. But Jacob's words failed to take the edge off her fear. Jinx had managed to call a hit on her FBI transport before escaping from custody. She had no doubt that if he wanted to, he could find a way to make it through the storm and come after her here, as well.

"And when the storm's over?" she asked. "He's not going to stop until I'm silenced."

"I say we worry about that when the time comes," Marci said.

"You're right." Tory drew in a deep breath while trying at the same time to shake the fear that had taken hold. "I'm safe for now, and I can't tell you how much I appreciate your generosity. All three of you."

"We're happy to help," Griffin said.

She forced herself to finish eating the rest of her stew—a family recipe that called for elk meat hunted on their land, she'd been told, passed down from Griffin's great-grandmother. While she sure would have enjoyed the meal if circumstances had been different, at the moment it was tasteless.

Marci stood from the table as soon as everyone had finished and caught her son's gaze. "Why don't the two of you go relax in the other room while your father and

I clean up? You both look exhausted. I have some cobbler with berries from our summer garden and vanilla ice cream, if you're interested."

Tory scooted her chair back from the table. "Let me at least help clean up first."

Marci waved away her request. "You go relax. I insist. Besides, I have the world's number-one dishwasher right here beside me."

Jacob's brow crinkled when he laughed. "How did I know that was coming?"

Tory looked to Griffin.

"It's not worth arguing with them," he said. "They always win."

"While you're at it," his mother continued, "try not to think too hard about what you can't remember. Doctor's orders."

Tory smiled. "Yes, ma'am."

"Go on into the living room," Griffin said. "I'll bring you some of the dessert."

She nodded, feeling spoiled but too tired to argue, and went to stand in front of the Christmas tree. She breathed in the scent of fresh pine from the lighted green tree that no doubt had come from the ranch. White lights flickered against multicolored glass ornaments. She'd hoped that sitting around the table with his family would jog her mind and bring up memories of Christmas dinners, birthday parties and anniversaries from her own past. She had to have experienced those things at some point growing up.

But whatever those memories were, they were still lost for the moment.

Two minutes later Griffin handed her a bowl of cobbler with ice cream and stood beside her at the tree. "You seem deep in thought. What are you thinking about?"

"The one thing I can't forget." She couldn't help but shake her head at the irony as she took a spoon from him. For someone who'd lost most of her memories, there was one she couldn't shake. "He's out there, Griffin. And his escape ups the stakes. He's going to come after me himself."

"Maybe, but if I were him, I'd forget about any witnesses and simply flee the country."

"Don't you think that's easier said than done?"

"Probably. But he's got to have plenty of money and resources to set himself up on some island and live out the rest of his days sitting in the sun."

Needing a distraction, she reached up and touched a glass snowman hanging on one of the branches. "I'm guessing you didn't pick this tree up at a local farm."

"No. Comes from right here. We always head out into the woods the day after Thanksgiving and find the perfect tree for my mom."

"It's beautiful," she said.

"Christmas is a pretty big deal around here, even now that we're all grown up."

"What do you do?" she asked.

He took a bite of his dessert. "Besides helping my mom with the decorations here, there's the annual Christmas parade and concert in town, and volunteering for the Giving Tree at church that helps families in our community who are in need."

"That all sounds fun."

"It is my favorite time of the year."

She followed him to the couch and sat next to him before sampling a bite of ice cream and berries. She knew she needed to relax, but her mind wouldn't stop working on the what-ifs.

"I'm guessing you're not really in the Christmas mood right now," he added.

"Not really. I keep thinking about the file we read through. It said that Jinx normally lets his soldiers handle all his dirty work," she told him. "It's one reason why the man has never been caught. But it also said that this time was different. He shot that couple himself. That must mean their deaths were personal. And what he didn't count on was having a witness."

"What are you thinking?" Griffin asked.

"I've been going over and over in my head about what you said about my having information he wants."

"And…"

"I still can't remember anything, but my gut tells me you're right." She set her dessert on her lap, her appetite soured. "I just can't pull up the information."

"My mom was right. Try not to think about it. I have a feeling the more you try to bring those memories to the surface, the harder it's going to be."

"Maybe, but it's the not knowing that makes me feel the most vulnerable. Like I've somehow stepped into a gunfight but I have nothing to defend myself. This is something I don't know how to deal with. I can't keep my brain from spinning."

"There is something else to consider."

She drew in a deep breath. "What's that?"

"My mom told me it's possible that memory loss can

come from witnessing something traumatic. Like the car wreck and the agents being shot."

Tory worked to process what he said as she tried digging into the cobbler, not liking the implications. "Meaning I'm too afraid to remember."

"It's a possibility."

"I guess I'd like to think I'm stronger than that. I work in the emergency room, which goes to reason that I've witnessed a lot of traumatic situations."

Whether it was true or not, the thought made her feel as if she were weak. As if her mind couldn't handle what she had seen and had literally shut down. As far as she was concerned, the lump on the back of her head sounded like a more realistic option. But either way, her memories still refused to surface.

Griffin shook his head. "This has nothing to do with how strong you are. That's how God created your mind. A kind of protection when having to face something traumatic. Maybe things are different because, this time, the trauma was directed toward you."

She took another bite of the tart berries with the sweet ice cream. Like, witnessing an agent shot dead in front of her. Was that enough to erase her memories? She might not know for sure, but there was one thing she was certain of. Not being able to do anything about it made her feel helpless.

"Your parents are sweet—and your mom is such a good cook," she said. "I just hope they know how much I appreciate their taking me in."

"They enjoy company and are known to spoil their boys every once in a while."

"I'll admit I don't mind being spoiled a bit. And this is delicious."

"I told you you'd feel safe here. I want you to feel safe here."

She caught the intensity in Griffin's eyes and wondered why he was doing this. In reality, he didn't have to. She was pretty certain that guarding an FBI witness wasn't anywhere in his job description, and he could have easily passed it on to someone else. But, for some reason, she was glad he had taken the job. Because there was something about his presence that was calming and reassuring. Something about him that made her want to pull back the layers and find out everything there was to know about him.

Especially since uncovering exactly who she was seemed impossible at the moment.

"It's strange to think I don't have any family," she said, giving in to the need to probe beyond the surface. "There's got to be someone out there who's worried about me. Someone who knew what I was doing. I don't even know if I have a significant other."

Her gaze shifted back to the tree with a dozen presents already beneath it. Had she put up a tree back home? Were there presents underneath it? How could she forget something like that?

"Have any more memories surfaced?" he asked.

"Not really. I went over the FBI file half a dozen times before dinner, certain something would jog my memory, but so far it's still just a bunch of foggy details, with nothing more than a few impressions." She took another bite of her dessert. "Though I've learned that I like ice cream and berry cobbler way too much."

"I'd think something was seriously wrong with you if you didn't."

"Funny." She couldn't help but notice how his eyes smiled and how his brown eyes had flecks of gold in them.

"And I've learned a few more things about you," he said.

"Like?" She sat back and waited for him to continue.

"You're strong. You have a sense of humor." Griffin paused. "And you're beautiful."

"I'm guessing I blush at compliments, as well."

He smiled back, but she didn't like the way he stirred her heart. She couldn't remember what she ate for breakfast yesterday, let alone if there was someone else in her life. This definitely wasn't the time or place to be feeling the tug of an attraction. All she was going to end up with was a broken heart. And somehow— despite everything she'd forgotten—she knew she'd had at least one of those.

Griffin studied Tory for a moment while she dug into her dessert, wondering why he'd said something so…personal. She was beautiful, but to say it out loud?

Still, there was something different about her from most women he met—something he couldn't quite put his finger on. Despite the alarming situation she was being forced to deal with, she was managing to hold herself together better than he'd expected. With her medical training, it made sense. She was used to making decisions in the middle of a crisis situation, but having a man who was wanted by the FBI after you brought things to a whole other level. Those feelings of fear and vulnerability were amplified with her memories suppressed. Being attracted to someone who couldn't remember who they were seemed ridiculous.

He needed a distraction and he had a feeling so did she.

"How about a movie?" he said. "It might keep your mind off of all of this for a while."

And keep his mind off the woman sitting next to him.

She took another bite. "For some reason, I don't think I'm a huge movie fan, but I think I'd like that tonight."

"Good. My parents have a huge selection of DVDs. What's your favorite?" He sat back, wanting to take back the question. "I'm sorry."

"Forget it. Why don't you choose?"

He set his dessert on the coffee table, grabbed one of the movies he knew his mother loved and slipped it into the DVD player. Why did he keep forgetting he wasn't there to get to know her? This was a job, nothing more. Besides, how was he supposed to get to know her when she couldn't remember her past? Even if it did eventually come back, his job was just until the FBI detail got here.

Halfway through the movie, they added a big bowl of buttered popcorn. When the final credits rolled, he realized she was leaning against his shoulder.

"Are you still awake?" he asked.

She nodded then yawned "I saw the ending, but think I missed part of it."

"I learned you have a cute snore."

"Very funny." She laughed. "I learned I like romantic comedies. Especially Christmas ones."

"I figured something intense wasn't going to be a good choice considering that the point was for you to forget everything that's going on, so I guess we accomplished that."

"Agreed." She scooted a few inches away and turned to him. "But to be honest, forgetting things hasn't exactly been an issue since the accident."

Griffin frowned, wanting to kick himself for his insensitivity. "I'm sorry, I didn't mean—"

"It's okay." She shot him a smile. "I'm teasing."

He let out a low chuckle. "You might have lost your memory, but like I said earlier, definitely not your sense of humor."

"What I really should be saying is thank you."

"For what?"

"For helping me get my mind off all of this, even if it was just for a couple hours—and even if I fell asleep. I have a feeling that the next few days if not weeks are going to be tough. But in the meantime, I can't imagine a homier safe house."

He turned off the TV and the Christmas lights, grabbed the half-empty bowl of popcorn and headed toward the kitchen. "I can't guarantee that the FBI is going to treat you to a movie and popcorn every night, but while you're here we can afford to indulge some."

He stopped midsentence, realizing what he was thinking. For some crazy reason he wished she were staying here—not just until the storm was over, but until he knew she was completely safe. And he wanted to be the one to ensure she stayed safe. But that wasn't going to happen. She'd only be here until the storm passed and the FBI could get her out, then he'd get back to his normal life.

And reality.

He turned off the kitchen light and started upstairs with her.

"The house is beautiful." She ran her hand across the wooden banister as they walked up the stairs. "When was it built?"

"My grandfather built the original structure back in the early 1900s, but my father continued to add on. He put in the second story back in the seventies, added a back porch and most recently put in a gun room for safety."

She glanced at the vaulted door at the end of the hallway. "So he's a serious hunter?"

"Hunter...collector. He had the vault put in a few months ago. His first grandchild—and any future grandchildren—was his main motivator, though he's been talking about doing it for years. If you're interested in hunting, he's the man people come to. I might be biased, but he and my grandfather are experts on not just hunting but survival and really anything outdoors. He loves this land and knows how to adapt to whatever comes."

She stood quiet for a minute in front of the guest room.

"You okay?"

"Yeah. I'm fine. Just tired. I love hearing you talk of family, but it makes me wonder about mine."

"The memories will come."

She nodded. "I hope so."

"Do you need anything else?"

"I don't think so. I have my bag from the agents' car and your mother helped me get settled."

"Good. But if you end up needing something—

anything at all—during the night, I'm just down the hall."

"I'm sure I'll be fine."

A moment later she turned around and slipped into her room.

He stared at the closed door a few seconds then made a tour of the house, ensuring all the doors and windows were locked. His parents had gone to bed an hour ago, but he had a feeling he wasn't going to get much sleep.

The wind was still howling outside and the snow continued to lay a thick blanket on the ground, which meant he couldn't imagine someone coming after her now. Not in this weather. But he still wasn't going to take any chances. His brother Caden and the ranch hands were already on alert to anything out of the ordinary. And the local sheriff's department had their deputies on call, as well.

If Jinx did manage to track her down and come after her, they were going to be ready.

He checked the mudroom door then stopped and moved closer to the window. Something shifted outside near the barn and he was sure it wasn't simply the wind. He grabbed his heavy coat and gloves off the hanging rack, along with a flashlight, then put his service weapon in his holster. If Jinx and his men were foolish enough to try to fight this storm, he was going to make sure they lost.

The wind howled around him as he stepped outside and quickly shut the door behind him. Bitter cold slashed his cheeks, sending shivers up his spine. Steeling his breath, he headed for the barn. Shadows moved in the wind, but that wasn't what he'd seen. Some-thing—someone was out there.

He held out his weapon as he approached the barn. "Turn around slowly and put your hands on your head."

He shone his flashlight into the shadows. "Caden?"

His brother stepped up in front of him. "What are you doing out here?"

"Just checking things over one last time. I can't see those guys coming after her tonight, but saw someone moving around and had to check it out. What are you doing?"

Caden let out a low laugh. "I think we're both a bit on edge. It hasn't been that long since Gabby's and Liam's lives were in danger, and now this…"

Griffin stepped into the shelter of the barn behind his brother. "I have to admit, this situation has me rat-tled and they've crossed my mind once or twice the past few hours."

Caden shot him a smile. "Gabby fell in love with Liam during all of that. The same thing could happen to you."

"Seriously? There's a killer after the woman I'm protecting, and you're thinking about matchmaking?" Griffin frowned. "I'm not doing this because I think she's beautiful or charming. I'm just doing my job."

"If you say so."

"Caden, you can't seriously be going there. I don't even know her."

His brother let out a low chuckle. "You know I'm just kidding, though it has been a while since you've been in a relationship. I'm just thinking of your happi-ness. Mom told me Tory's both beautiful and charming."

Griffin headed into one of the stalls to check the supply of feed, even though it wasn't his job.

Caden followed him, stopping in the doorway. "I'm sorry."

"Forget it. That was a long time ago. I just haven't found what I'm looking for."

"What are you looking for?"

He headed into the next stall, wanting to ignore the question. Wanting to ignore the entire topic.

"You're not exactly one to give relationship advice."

The four brothers had fought like cats and dogs growing up, but in the end they would have sacrificed anything for each other. Caden and his fiancée had broken off their engagement the night before their wedding. He'd never told Griffin the entire story of what had happened, and Griffin had never pushed. Just like he'd never shared with Caden all the details of losing Lilly.

But none of that mattered right now.

"What I just said crossed the line," Griffin said.

"Forget it. It's just that you've just seemed…lost lately."

Griffin stepped out of the stall. "I'm fine. Busy at work and church… There's nothing to complain about."

"But that's not always enough, is it?"

"I just…" He stopped. Wasn't that the same question he'd been asking himself? What was he looking for?

Satisfied the horses had what they needed for the night, Griffin buttoned the top of his coat. He needed to get back to the house to ensure everything was okay there.

"If things were different, I might not mind getting to know her, but she can't remember much more than her name, which makes it a bit hard." He stopped just inside the doorway leading outside and rested his hands on his hips. "I think the stress of all of this is taking more of a toll than I realized."

"She's going to be fine," Caden said, heading toward the door with him. "She's got you as her guardian."

He was cold and tired and needed to get a good night's sleep if he was going to be able to do his job. "We both should get some sleep."

"Agreed. I'll see you in the morning."

Griffin walked back to the house and made another sweep of the perimeter, knowing he wouldn't sleep tonight. While the chances of Jinx or his men facing this storm seemed slim, he still wasn't going to dismiss the possibility. That meant he couldn't put his guard down.

He glanced up at the window of the room where Tory was sleeping then shifted his gaze toward the shadows in the living room. This time he wasn't imagining anything. Someone had broken into the house.

FIVE

Tory woke with a start. After hours of not being able to sleep, she'd finally dozed off only to be jerked back awake. It was still dark outside and she had no idea what had startled her. She grabbed her phone to check the time. It was only half past twelve. Maybe she hadn't been asleep as long as she'd thought.

She crawled out of bed, shoved her feet into her thick slippers and then stopped in front of the window. Snow was falling and had already covered the ground with several inches. Griffin had been right. Jinx might have escaped, but he couldn't find her here. The authorities would catch him and all this would be over.

At least that's what she prayed would happen. Somehow she was pretty sure it wasn't going to be that easy.

If she testified, he'd send someone after her.

If she didn't testify, he'd go free and probably still send someone after her.

There was no way to win.

A memory flickered in the recesses of her mind as she headed out of her room, but she couldn't catch it. She'd head downstairs to get a drink then try to go back to sleep. Try to not dwell on the fact that her memories were locked up in a place she couldn't access.

She'd have to read the additional case files the FBI had sent over and, she hoped, uncover clues to what for now had been lost. But there was something unnerving about trying to find out who you were in a government file.

Another noise snapped her out of her thoughts. Someone was moving inside the house. The hairs on the back of her neck prickled, but she knew it was probably just Griffin or his parents. She drew in a deep breath, trying to slow her heart rate. It wasn't anything sinister. Like her, he was probably having trouble sleeping.

She dismissed the fear and headed down the main staircase and into the kitchen.

"Tory."

She spun around. "Griffin?"

A sigh of relief escaped her lips. She'd let her imagination take over but she'd been right. There was nothing to be afraid of.

"There are two men in the house," he whispered.

"What?"

The night-light in the living room went out, leaving them in darkness.

"They've cut the electricity."

Fear pressed against her chest. This couldn't be happening. She was supposed to be safe here. But now...

Griffin motioned for her to stay quiet as he grabbed her hand and pulled her across the kitchen toward the laundry room. "They're here in the house. Upstairs. I don't know how you managed to miss them, but I need you to come with me."

She went willingly, an indication in her mind of how

much she trusted him. But trust didn't take away the panic engulfing her. Jinx had no intention of simply disappearing. He wanted her dead and was willing to battle a storm to take her out.

She caught the glint of the handgun Griffin held as the moonlight streamed through the window and wondered how it had come to this. She was supposed to be safe here. A shelter in the storm until the FBI could retrieve her. She had to have known she was putting her life at risk when she'd decided to testify against a man like Jinx, but now she was risking Griffin's family's lives, too. She didn't want that. And she had no desire for him to put his life on the line to fight for her. But what other options did they have at this point?

He pulled her into the laundry room and shut the door behind them. She had a dozen questions to ask Griffin. Like, how were they going to escape? But all she really needed to know was that Jinx's men—and maybe Jinx himself—were here in the house and, with the storm in full force outside, escaping was going to be next to impossible.

How were they supposed to hide when there was nowhere to go?

Griffin released her hand and pulled out a handheld two-way radio. "Caden…we've got two intruders in the house."

"Where are you?"

"Downstairs in the laundry room."

"You need to get her to the safe room."

"That was my plan, but they're blocking it."

"Can you take them out?" Caden asked.

"Yes, but I could use some backup. I'd rather avoid someone getting hurt in a confrontation."

"What about Mom and Dad?"

"I haven't been able to get through to them."

"I'm on my way to the house now."

"Copy that."

She heard movement behind them. The door swung open, followed by a bright light and then everything went dark.

Tory grabbed Griffin's arm, though she couldn't see or hear anything. Someone pulled her up but she couldn't make out who it was. Was it Griffin or one of Jinx's men? She couldn't tell. Her ears were ringing and her heart pounded as her vision came back into focus. Someone grabbed her from behind but Griffin pounced on the man, forcing him to lose his grip. Free, she snatched an iron off the dryer and swung at a second man with everything she had. A moment later the man dropped to the ground.

Griffin grabbed her hand. "We need to get out of here. Can you run?"

"Yeah." She still wasn't sure where he planned to go, but she wasn't going to wait to find out.

He swung open the outside door and helped her down the porch stairs. The cold hit her like a freight train. She was wearing sweats, a long T-shirt and slippers with soles, but that wasn't enough to protect her from the freezing temperatures or the snow that was still falling. It wouldn't take long, exposed in this weather, to bring on the first stages of hypothermia.

She didn't question his decision as they headed for the barn, but there was no way they could take a horse out into this weather. That left them with no real escape as far as she could tell. But Griffin had a plan. He had to.

Her lungs hurt as she took in a breath. "Where are we going?"

"To the barn. We've got a couple snowmobiles there."

They crossed the gravel driveway that was now covered with several inches of white, the only light a sliver of moon reflecting off the falling snow. She had no idea what had happened to his parents, but she had a feeling that Jacob and Marci O'Callaghan could take care of themselves.

God, don't let anything happen to them, please...not because of me.

As Griffin opened the door, the wind whipped it out of his hand and slammed it against the barn wall. She heard something and turned around, catching movement out of the corner of her eye. The men had followed them outside.

"Griffin!"

One of the men tackled Griffin, shoving him against the wall of a stall. He let out a groan while a second man grabbed her, pinned her arms behind her and started dragging her across the floor. She fought back and pulled away from his grip, but he was too strong. She watched helplessly as the other man swung, plummeting his fists first into Griffin's rib cage then across his jaw.

This time Griffin didn't get up.

Her feet were numb and she was shaking from the bitter cold. She needed to do something. But she couldn't move. Couldn't think. They had Griffin now and there was nothing she could do to stop them.

"Should we leave him?" one of the men asked.

"No… Get him onto his feet. I have a feeling we're going to need them both. Keys are in the snowmobiles. We'll use them to get to the cabin."

Cabin? What cabin?

There was no time to figure out what they were planning. The man who had grabbed her quickly tied her hands in front of her with a long piece of twine he'd been carrying, before securing her to the bar on the back of the snowmobile. The second man aimed his gun at Griffin and ordered him to drive, before sliding in behind him, his gun still pointed at Griffin's head.

Seconds later both snowmobiles took off into the blistering storm, leaving her wondering why they hadn't just killed her. If Griffin was right, and they wanted information from her, what did they want?

The man sitting behind Griffin fired a round at the barn. She looked back and saw someone running toward them, but it didn't matter anymore. It was too late.

Griffin's head pounded as he drove the snowmobile and the frigid air filled his lungs. His chest hurt, making him wonder if he had a cracked rib, but all he could think about was Tory—and the instructions of the man behind him, pointing a gun at his head.

This wasn't supposed to have happened. He'd done everything he could think of to ensure her safety, including coordinating emergency plans with his parents, Caden and the local police, but the whole time he'd believed that the men wouldn't come until the storm died down. And if they did, he'd still have the advantage because he knew this land. Instead he'd underestimated their motivation and the risks they'd take. What worried him the most was that their plan had to be to kill her once they got what they wanted.

On top of that, not only had he failed to keep Tory safe, he had no idea if his parents were okay. Guilt engulfed him as he worked to focus on the surrounding terrain and a way out of this. Thankfully, he knew the ranch as well as his father, because he needed to know not only where they were right now, but where they were going. There had been a slight lull in the storm, but he knew it was supposed to hit with force again. That meant, if they'd planned their attack based on up-to-date information, they no doubt knew exactly where they were going. If he was right, he was pretty sure they also had a man inside the FBI.

They passed a familiar tower used to collect rainwater. That meant they were heading west, toward the only outbuilding in this direction, a structure used to store feed and other supplies for the outskirts of the ranch. But if that was their plan, then what? If they'd wanted him and Tory dead, they could have done that back at the ranch.

He'd been right. Their plan was to keep Tory alive, but only until they got whatever information they were after. In the meantime, he was going to be used as leverage to get her to talk. But what if she couldn't give them the answers they demanded? There was no way for them to know she had no memories of what she'd witnessed, or when those memories might come back. That left him with only one real option. He needed to get Tory away from the men now.

As soon as the trail widened, Griffin found what he was looking for. He steered the snowmobile over a slight rise that launched them several inches into the air before hitting the ground and skidding to an abrupt stop. A second later he yanked the other man off the snowmobile and onto the ground, slamming a fist into the back of his skull before grabbing for the man's gun.

The second snowmobile carrying Tory came to a stop behind him, but Griffin was ready. He pointed the gun at the second man. "Let her go!"

The driver jerked Tory in front of him, blocking Griffin's shot. "Get back on the snowmobile or she's dead."

"I thought your boss needed her alive," he shouted back.

The man he'd knocked out stumbled to his feet. "You have no idea what's really going on here. If it were up to me, I'd have ended this a long time ago. But our boss has his own agenda."

"What is it?"

"You'll find out soon enough." He motioned for Griffin to get back on the vehicle. "Try anything again and I'll forget about what the boss wants, and she'll be dead before she hits the ground. You'll both be dead."

Griffin hesitated then caught the fear in Tory's eyes. He was irritated. He'd taken a calculated risk and lost. If it were just him, he'd take the chance and fight back, but he couldn't put her life in any more jeopardy than it already was. Not here, anyway.

Fifteen minutes later they stopped in front of a supply structure and the men led them into the building by gunpoint. He glanced around the familiar ten-by-twelve filled with building supplies, feed and fencing materials. The thick walls kept out the wind and a small heater provided just enough warmth to keep off the chill. The only positive thing about the situation was that the inside was warmer than outside.

He turned to Tory. "Are you okay?"

She nodded, but he could tell she wasn't. Her face was red from the cold. He didn't know which was worse, the cold or the fear that had to have settled around her.

"I—"

"Shut up." One of the men stopped in front of him and pulled off the ski mask he'd been wearing.

Griffin's jaw slackened. "Max?"

"You know him?" Tory asked.

"He's one of our old ranch hands who was fired for stealing."

Max frowned. "Wouldn't have had to if your father paid a fair wage."

"He pays more than a fair wage and you know it. But you got caught."

Max shrugged. "Maybe things are about to turn around for me. Ran into Jimmy here at the diner today. Found out his boss is willing to pay me a whole lot more."

"You'd rather work for a man who murders his employees than one who treats them fair?" Griffin asked.

"Enough. Both of you." Jimmy shouted at Griffin, "You're only here for one reason and that's not for giving orders but to ensure she talks." The cold had brought out the red in a two-inch scar across the man's temple as he turned to Tory. "Which you will do because, trust me, the alternative isn't going to be pretty if you want your bodyguard here to live."

"Don't hurt him, please. Just tell me what you want from me."

He thrust Tory backward into a wood chair, while Max did the same to Griffin.

I don't know what to do here, God.

He glanced at the door. If he could buy them some time and the snow hadn't already covered their tracks, there was a chance Caden and the other men would be able to track them down. The only problem was, they had the only snowmobiles on the property.

"You don't have to do this," Griffin began. "Because you know that in the end you'll be arrested, and it won't be Jinx who goes to prison for kidnapping and assault, it will be you. Is that what you want? To take the fall for another man?"

While he waited for their response, he studied the expression of the man closest to him. He was clearly loyal to Jinx. Griffin wasn't sure what motivated him, but there was definitely some history there. These men were willing to kill on another man's orders. Men who lost all sense of conscience and the ability to see between right and wrong. How did he fight that?

Jimmy took a step forward. "You don't know what you're talking about."

"Really? Because I think you know I'm telling the truth. Your boss will get away with murder—and now with the kidnapping of a deputy. He will get away with this, like he always does, because he knows you'll take the fall if it goes wrong. But he won't.

"The authorities know you can't have gotten far in this storm. They will find us here, and when they do, you'll be the ones going to prison. Is that really what you want to happen? Why go down for a man who doesn't care if you live or die? He's the kind of man who has no problems risking your life by sending you out into a storm to clean up his mess."

Planting the seeds of doubt was his last defense.

Jimmy leaned down and slammed a fist into his stomach. Griffin groaned at the sharp jab of pain at the impact, realizing that appealing to this man's conscience wasn't going to work.

"Don't…please…" Tory tried to scoot closer to him. "Leave him alone and tell me what you want from me."

"Fine. Because I'm tired of all the talk and wasting time." Jimmy squatted down in front of her. "I want to know who the other witness is you're protecting."

Griffin watched Tory's jaw go slack. He'd figured they wanted information, but another witness? The FBI had specifically told him that Tory was the only witness in this case. Why would they have misled him about something like that?

He watched as Tory blinked back the confusion. So that was the information they'd been looking for. Someone else had been there with her that day. Who? A friend? A boyfriend? But if that was true, then why hadn't it been mentioned in the FBI file? For that matter, what else about that file had been a lie? If there was another witness, the only thing that made sense was that Tory must have either insisted on leaving out the second witness as a bargaining chip when she'd agreed to help the FBI or the FBI didn't know. He could tell she had no idea because she still couldn't remember what had happened that day. But one thing was clear. She had to have been protecting someone.

But who?

Jimmy leaned forward and spittle flew out of his mouth as he spoke. "Answer my question. Who's the other witness?"

Tory bit the edge of her lip. "I don't know."

"You don't know?"

He signaled at Max, who punched Griffin, this time against his mouth. A drop of blood trickled down his lip and dropped onto the wooden floor. Griffin's heart raced. Unless he could find a way out, this wasn't going to end well for either of them.

Tory scooted forward. "Don't…please don't hurt him."

Jimmy set his hands against the armrest and leaned in even closer to her face. "Then tell me what I want to know. Because if you don't, he's expendable."

Griffin's gut cinched. They were walking a fine line. If she told him the truth about her memory, she was going to take away any leverage the men might have had in keeping them alive.

SIX

Tory felt her stomach clench as Jimmy's stale breath pressed toward her face. Her mind scrambled to make sense of what he was saying, because she couldn't grasp what he was asking her. There had been another witness? Was that even possible?

Unless...

She turned her face away as everything suddenly started coming into place. Griffin was right. They didn't want her dead because they wanted something from her. The encounter with the agents *had* been an extraction, not an attempt to kill her. For some reason, Jinx and his men were afraid of what she knew. They still needed one piece of evidence, and that piece of evidence changed everything. Except there was something else vital they didn't know. If what they were saying was true, she had no idea who had been on that trail with her that day.

"Answer my question," Jimmy repeated. "Who was with you that day?"

Tory felt her heart slam against the wall of her chest from a fresh wave of adrenaline. She had no idea what to answer. If she didn't have the information they wanted, what reason did they have to keep them alive? She glanced at Griffin. His lip quivered from the pain, but she couldn't read his expression. Somehow she needed to buy time and the only way to do that was to tell the truth.

"I don't know who was with me that day," she finally said.

"You don't know?" Jimmy took a step back and laughed. "That's your answer? Do you really think that playing stupid is the right call here? If you're not careful, you're going to give your friend a death sentence, because apparently we haven't motivated you enough."

Max swung his fist back to hit Griffin.

"Stop! Please. Don't hurt him. I'm telling the truth."

Max froze midswing. "Then I'll ask you nicely one final time. Who was with you that day? Who's the second witness?"

Tory lowered her head. "I can't remember."

"What do you mean you can't remember?"

"In the crash… I lost my memories. I have amnesia."

"Amnesia." Max's hand dropped to his side. "Are you kidding me?"

She kept her eyes trained on a row of blue pipes laid out on a wooden shelf and tried to stay calm. "The memories should come back, but for now… I don't remember that day. Don't remember what I saw."

"You're lying."

She was uncertain if she'd played the right card, but there was no going back now. "I'm not lying. My memories are there, I just can't access them."

Max's frown deepened. "She's stalling, Jimmy—"

"I'm not. It's the truth. My memories are slowly returning, but I can't force them. It's going to take time."

"Unfortunately, time is something we don't have." Jimmy blew out a sharp breath. "You need to stop playing games and tell me who was there. Because if you try to protect them, someone's going to get hurt. Starting with the deputy."

"She's telling the truth." Griffin caught her gaze. "She can't remember."

Jimmy shifted his gun back to Griffin. "And I'm supposed to believe that she conveniently forgot who was with her that day? I'm not stupid."

Her head pounded. She had to find a way to convince them. All they needed was time for Griffin's brothers and the others to find them. Despite the storm, they couldn't be that far behind.

Please God...there has to be a way out of this...

"In the accident, I hit my head," she said. "My memories are coming back slowly, but for the most part they're hazy. For now, I can't remember that day."

Jimmy leaned back against a stack of boxes. "Some witness you're going to make for the prosecution. So, they will come back. When it's...convenient for you. Like, when you're on that witness stand?"

"I don't know when they'll come back."

Her panic shifted between not telling them what they wanted and what would happen if she did remember and told them. More than likely, they'd kill her and Griffin either way.

But who was the witness she was protecting? There had to be a way to remember.

"What *do* you remember?" Jimmy asked.

"The two of you killed the agents. I recognize your

clothes." She was surprised by her bold response but she was too tired to play games.

"And before that?"

She pressed her lips together. Her headache was getting worse. Trying to force her to remember wasn't going to help.

"Why do you believe there was a second witness?" she asked. "There wasn't one in the files we saw."

"I was there," Jimmy said. "I saw you and another woman on the rise above us."

"But you don't know who it was."

"You're catching on. And our boss—Jinx—let's just say he doesn't like to leave loose ends."

Tory tried to search her memories—the few she had—for any mention of a second witness in the FBI report, but she knew it wasn't there. Why? According to the file, she didn't have any living family. No parents or siblings. So that left a friend. That made sense. It was unlikely she would have gone hiking alone.

Who was she trying to protect? And why wasn't there any mention of it in the files?

Unless... Griffin believed there was a leak. That leak had to be the person who'd divulged the route her escort had taken. Had the FBI feared there was a mole? Someone under the influence of Jinx in the FBI? If so, it might make sense that they'd left out information in the file to protect that person. But who?

There was one other option. What if she'd never told the FBI about a second witness?

"How did you know about my detail?" she asked. "Seems like if you have that kind of inside information, you'd also know who the second witness is."

"Jinx has his…inside sources, but even that has limits."

So there was a leak. Someone who, apparently, Jinx was paying to get his information. Had she made some kind of deal with the FBI, so that information had been scrubbed?

"What do you want me to do?" she asked.

Max leaned forward, close enough that she could feel his breath on her cheek, and she fought the desire to gag. "I want you to tell me the truth."

"Give her some time," Griffin interrupted. "Her memories are coming back slowly, but if you try to force her to remember, it will only make it harder. You need to give her some time."

Jimmy took a step back and nodded at Max. "We need to talk."

The men stepped into the small, adjacent room, keeping the door cracked and leaving her alone with Griffin for the first time.

"I'm so sorry." Anxiety grew as the reality of the situation seeped through her. "This wasn't supposed to have happened and now—"

"Stop." He angled his body toward her as much as he could. "You have nothing to be sorry about. And maybe this is better. They need to know who was there with you, but once you tell them, they won't need either of us anymore. So you've bought us some time."

"And if they're not willing to wait? There's no telling what they'll do to you." Tory glanced toward the door, trying not to hyperventilate. "We need to get out of here, because even if I do remember who was with me, I can't tell them."

She kept working on undoing the binding holding her hands together behind her, but instead of loosening, they were rubbing her wrists raw. What other option did they have? The only way she could see them getting out of this was to escape. But how were they going to do that against two armed men and a storm raging in the background? Somehow they needed to find a way.

She tried to swallow the lump in her throat but couldn't. "They're going to kill us, Griffin."

"They seem pretty desperate to find the other witness. I don't think they'll do anything rash, and that should be enough to give us a chance to get out of here."

"I want to remember and yet, if I do, I put someone else's life in danger." She drew in a slow breath, wishing there was an out. "How can I do that again? It would be a death sentence. The FBI agents…you…whoever the second witness is—"

"Stop. We're going to find a way out of this."

"How?"

She squeezed her eyes shut, trying to force her mind to remember. It had to have been someone she was close to. Someone she cared about and wanted to protect. Someone she had intended to ensure stayed safe. But what about Griffin? She couldn't sacrifice his life to protect someone else.

The picture of the agent's face as he died in the front seat of the car surfaced again, cemented in her mind unlike all the other memories she couldn't access. She couldn't shake his image or his dying words.

They're after you.

Go…

And now they had her.

* * *

Griffin worked to undo the cord binding his hands, wishing he had answers to her questions. He was responsible for her, but somehow he'd failed to keep her safe. The rough cord dug into his skin, leaving his wrists raw, but he barely felt it. He wasn't worried what they'd do to him. He was worried about her.

His own memories rushed to the surface. Memories of Lilly's face… The last time he'd seen her… And the funeral. Memories he'd tried for a decade to forget that were now propelling him to the one place he didn't want to go. He'd told Caden that he wasn't the one to be giving relationship advice, but if Griffin were honest, he was the one who had let the past keep him from moving forward. It hadn't just been the reality of losing Lilly that had paralyzed him. It was the fact that he hadn't been able to save her. And the ensuing guilt he'd never been able to get rid of.

His gaze shifted to Tory, helping to pull him back into the present. This might be a different situation, but he still felt responsible and needed to focus on getting them out of there. Because as much as he trusted that his brothers and the ranch hands were doing everything they could do to track them down, he knew he couldn't wait for them. His only option was to get loose and take the men down.

"You okay?" she asked.

"Yeah. Just formulating a plan."

"What do you think they're going to do?"

"I'm not sure they know what to do right now. You've thrown them for a loop in telling them you can't remember who was there."

"I hope that ends up being a good thing." She drew in a deep breath. "Can I ask you something?"

He nodded, wishing they were talking under different circumstances. That they were sitting back at the ranch house in front of the fireplace with her head on his shoulder...

He shoved away the thought.

"In your job," she began, "have you ever been afraid for your life or the lives of people you loved?"

"Yeah...a couple times."

Tory caught his gaze and frowned, making him wonder if his face revealed too much. "If my question was too personal..."

"It's fine."

"I just... I know that I'm here because I was trying to protect someone, someone I cared about, and now, even though I don't know who it is, I'm terrified they're going to find her. And I have no idea how to stop them."

He watched a silent tear slide down her face and felt his heart break. She didn't deserve to be in a situation like this. She'd tried to do the right thing and now faced losing everything.

"Can I ask what happened when someone you loved was in danger?" she asked.

He worked his way back to her question. "I was the mediator for a hostage situation a few months ago that involved my brother and Gabby, the woman who's now his wife. Long story short, someone kidnapped her little girl to use her as leverage. Thankfully, they made it out safely, but it was a terrifying situation for all of us."

He should tell her about Lilly. She had been his real reason for becoming who he was today, but that was a story for another day. It had changed him. Made him stronger on the one hand, more vulnerable on the other.

"That's horrible and so personal," she said. "I can't imagine how you deal with life-and-death situations day after day. I admire your dedication."

He brushed off the compliment. "You do the same thing. Saving people. Bringing life into the world."

"Yes, but it's different. Most of the time it's a medical emergency, not someone trying to kill them. This…" She looked toward the door where the men were still talking. "I don't know how to deal with this."

"If I'm honest, most of the time my work is boring stuff. Routine traffic violations and parking tickets. Dealing with a few tourists who're being too rowdy." He needed to shift the conversation. He kept working to loosen the cords so he could move, then he glanced at the door, thankful the men were still talking—more than likely to Jinx. "And I don't normally get kidnapped and stuck in a room with a beautiful woman."

"Very funny."

"I was actually being serious, but as long as you think I'm funny, I have a short repertoire of jokes if you'd like to hear them."

He caught a hint of smile from her lips, which was exactly what he'd been going for.

"Something tells me you're a glass-half-full kind of guy," she said.

"It's usually better than the alternative."

At least he sounded more positive than he felt. The men's voices had risen and he assumed they were asking Jinx what they should do.

"I'm sorry," he said. "I'm not trying to make light of this."

He was doing what he always did. Using humor to avoid the harsh reality. What would she think if she knew the truth about him? That one of his looming failures in life had been not saving the woman he'd once loved.

"I never thought you were," she said, interrupting his thoughts. "You said this wasn't my fault. Well, it isn't your fault, either."

He let out a low chuckle. "Maybe we need to stop blaming ourselves then, and instead find a way out of this. You're a resourceful woman. You've proven that. And I know this terrain…far better than they do. If we can untie ourselves and get out of this storage shed, we'll have a chance."

"Okay." His words seemed to put determination back in her eyes. "Where would we go in this storm? The wind's still howling, it's probably snowing, and there's way over a foot of snow out there. What are our options?"

"There are snowmobiles out there and the men can't stay awake forever."

He caught the look of fear in her eyes. "You're going to try to take them down?"

"That's the only way out of this. There's a chance Caden will find us, but if he doesn't—"

"I know, but still… How are we supposed to do that?"

Griffin knew what she was thinking. The men were armed and he had no way to defend himself. But neither did he think that he had a choice. He might die trying, but if he did nothing, he'd probably end up dead anyway.

"Okay, but we still need to be practical." She inhaled a deep breath then slowly released it. "If we do make it out of here, where do we go? Neither of us is dressed for a blizzard. And these men? What if they follow us?"

"I need you to trust me, Tory. We'll deal with one problem at a time."

She nodded but he could tell by the fear in her eyes that she wasn't convinced.

"I spent my life here, which gives me the advantage." He shot her a smile. "And on top of that, I've got a pretty good left hook."

"I've seen that, but I think you're going to need a lot more than a left hook to take those men out."

He tried to downplay her comment. "I might have a few more tricks up my sleeve."

"Well then, it sounds as if I have nothing to worry about."

"I don't want you to worry, but I am going to need you to be a part of my plan." He could tell from her face that he hadn't completely convinced her. He knew it wasn't going to be without risk. The men had taken his gun out of his holster and patted him down for weapons, but they hadn't checked everywhere.

That was going to be their downfall.

SEVEN

She hated Griffin's plan. It was far too risky, but she knew that the alternative—sitting here and playing things out on their captors' terms—wasn't exactly an option, either. Her loss of memory had clearly thrown them off, which might be to her advantage, but that wasn't going to be enough. Because no matter what the men demanded from her, they weren't going to get the answers they wanted. At least not now.

Tory watched Griffin pull a knife out of his boot then shifted her gaze to the door in case the men decided to come back. The first step was to get loose. Then they'd worry about what happened next.

She leaned forward. "How much longer till you're free?"

"A minute…maybe two. I finally got loose enough to get to the knife, but now I need to cut the rope."

Ten seconds later the men stepped into the room and slammed the door behind them.

They didn't have a few more minutes.

Griffin pulled his hands back up where they'd been, giving no indication he had a knife. Her heart raced faster.

Now they were going to have to wait. And, in the meantime, deal once again with the men who'd grabbed them.

Jimmy shoved his cell phone into his pocket as he stepped up in front of her. "Jinx isn't happy with your answers."

She stared at the man. What did he want her to say? Even if she did remember, did he really think she was just going to reveal the truth? It was a standoff she knew she couldn't win.

"Did you tell anyone at the FBI who was with you that day?" Jimmy asked. "Because either you lied to them, or you made a deal to keep the second witness out of the file."

She met his gaze, praying he didn't tear into Griffin again. "I don't know."

"Well, you might need to think about it then, because Jinx doesn't believe you."

She let out a soft gasp. "I don't care what he believes, I'm telling the truth. I don't remember."

"And you're sure that's what you want to tell Jinx?"

She nodded.

"Unfortunately, you're going to end up regretting your decision. Since you refuse to be cooperative, there's a new plan. Jinx is coming here."

"In this storm?"

"Think about it… Jinx needs somewhere to lay low and this is the last place anyone would look because of the storm. Max here tells me that there's a trail that comes in from the north side of the property that leads here and should be passable with snowmobiles." Jimmy glanced at the door. "And it's as good a place as any to hole up till this crazy storm passes. Our tracks are long covered up and they'd never think of looking for us here, right under their noses. They're going to expect him to get as far away as possible."

Tory tried to keep her expression neutral but was sure she was failing. She was terrified.

"In the meantime…" he said. "You better hope and pray your memory comes back. Because when he arrives, he's going to expect an answer. And if you don't give him one…your friend will die."

"No—"

"This isn't a game. If I were you, I'd think about cooperating, and the sooner, the better."

And if she still couldn't remember? She might have bought them some time, but was it going to be enough? She had no idea how long it would take for Jinx to show up. She glanced at Griffin. One thing was clear. They had no choice now. They needed to get out before Jinx arrived. Unfortunately it looked like Jimmy and Max were prepared to wait it out.

The men settled in the corner of the room at an old table, drinking coffee out of a thermos and playing cards. Her back ached and her wrists felt raw from being tied behind her, but as much as she worked at the cords, she couldn't get them loose. Even if Griffin did manage to undo his bindings, she was worried about him. If he had any broken ribs from the beating he'd taken, their escape was going to be more complicated.

She started praying again, something that seemed so natural.

I've never felt so lost, God. Never felt so scared. I need…we need Your help.

She could tell by the determined set of his chin that

Griffin was still working to cut through the rope. His knife clanked onto the floor. He automatically moved his foot on top of it, blocking it from their captor's view. Her heart stilled as she looked across the room at the men. Griffin's back arched. She lifted up another prayer.

"What's going on?" Max started to get up.

"Nothing... I must have fallen asleep and jerked awake. It's not exactly comfortable sitting in this position."

Jimmy waved him back into the chair. "Leave them be. It's your turn."

Max hesitated then sat before throwing down his cards.

"I'm loose." Griffin said under his breath. "See if you can undo your hands." He managed to scoot the knife toward her with his foot.

She leaned over and grabbed it with her fingers. The men still weren't paying attention. Wind howled through the roof, covering up their movements, but she had to be careful.

She froze as Jimmy got up and moved toward them for another cup of coffee. But he still wasn't paying attention to them.

A minute later she was free. She handed Griffin back the knife. Griffin nodded at her then counted to three. He stood and threw his knife, landing it with precision in Max's shoulder. At the same time, she grabbed one of the metal pipes and swung it across the back of Jimmy's head. He let out a groan then slumped onto the floor.

Griffin shouted at her. "Throw me the rope."

She grabbed a length of the rope that had secured her only moments before, trying to ignore the sick feeling spreading through her. She might not remember the details of her day job, but she knew her business was helping people, not hurting them. Still, it amazed her how survival mode kicked in when her life—and the life of someone else—was on the line. It only took a matter of seconds for Griffin to secure Max while she stood over Jimmy with the pipe pressing into his back. Griffin then quickly bound Jimmy's hands and feet, ensuring they wouldn't get away.

"I would have thought you'd have done a better job patting me down," Griffin said.

"You fool, Max," Jimmy groaned, and turned onto his side. "I told you to make sure he didn't have any weapons on him."

Max didn't reply, but there was something else bothering her. Blood pooled beneath Jimmy's head where she'd hit him.

"I need to stop the bleeding," she said.

"Fine, but hurry," Griffin said. "We need to get out of here."

She grabbed an old rag lying on one of the shelves and pressed it against the wounds.

Jimmy gritted his teeth. "You're the most humane escaped kidnapping victim I've ever seen."

He groaned as she rolled him over so she could get a closer look at the injury. The cut was deep, but it didn't look like it was deep enough to cause serious, long-term damage.

"You're going to need stiches, but you'll live for now. From this, anyway. I'm not sure about your day job."

"We need to get out of here, Tory. The storm sounds like it has slowed down for the moment, but it's still not going to be easy driving through it."

"Give me a minute…"

"We need to go, Tory. He'll be fine. We'll grab enough clothing to keep us warm, then get as far away as possible."

Griffin drew in a breath and felt the frigid air fill his lungs. He couldn't believe they'd made it this far, but he wasn't ready to celebrate yet. Despite the storm raging outside, Jinx was on his way and the last thing he wanted was an encounter with the man. That meant what he had to focus on right now was getting Tory to safety.

He tried to ignore the pain pulsing across his rib cage and reminded himself that it could have been far worse. He was fortunate to be alive. He'd just have to put up with the pain until they got to town and he could see a doctor. The last thing he wanted was for Tory to worry about him. He didn't have time to give in to the pain and let it slow them down.

He took the coat she handed him, then grabbed the two guns he'd confiscated. Before they left, he quickly checked the bound men one last time, not wanting to take any chances that they could get loose and be able to follow.

"This won't work." The man pulled on the binding. "Jinx is on his way and I promise you, he'll track you until he finds you. And when he does…he won't be near as nice as I was."

"If I were you, I'd stick to worrying about what Jinx is going to do when he realizes you haven't done your job. From what I've heard, he doesn't deal well with people who don't do what they're told."

Griffin took the gloves she'd collected, then checked to make sure she was going to be warm enough.

"You look like a snowman," he teased.

The padded coat was at least two sizes too big for her. "Very funny."

"But a cute snowman." He reached out and pulled the scarf up around her cheeks to cover them. "I'll have the sheriff send someone here via snowmobile and lock up these guys. It's going to be over soon."

Tory nodded, but he could tell she wasn't convinced. She was thinking that Jinx was out there somewhere, on his way. But he'd meant what he said. This was going to be over soon. And he'd ensure they won.

Stepping outside was like entering a frozen tundra. The snow had tapered off some, but the icy wind sent chills down his spine. It had snowed at least another three or four inches since they'd been inside the storage shed, and the snowmobile was now covered.

He handed her the brush he'd grabbed inside the door. "If you'll start scraping off the snowmobile, I need to do a quick check before getting the engine started."

"What about their cell phones?"

"I'm just going to smash them," he said. "Without a passcode we can't get into them, plus we can't risk Jinx using them to track us. On top of that, there's no service this far out."

He quickly made sure the skis on the snowmobile weren't frozen to the ground, then checked that the back wasn't frozen. He gave the machine some gas, then cranked the engine.

Nothing.

He tried again as the frigid wind whipped through his clothes. This time the engine roared to life. He sent up a prayer of thanks, made sure Tory was settled, then took off down the snow-packed path.

She wrapped her arms tighter around his waist. "How far to the house?"

"At least twenty, maybe thirty, minutes."

The falling snow had transformed the ranch into a winter wonderland, making him wish he could share it with her in different circumstances. Especially now at Christmastime. There were traditions he somehow knew she'd enjoy, like cutting down a Christmas tree, listening to Christmas music and enjoying his mother's cooking.

He reined in his thoughts then quickly took his foot off the gas and slowed down. A tree with a large trunk blocked the path. He looked for alternatives, but there was no way they were going to get past the obstacle.

Griffin weighed his options. Going around meant at least an extra thirty minutes. He glanced back at Tory. Already her cheeks were bright red from the cold. He'd pulled up her scarf to cover her face better, but it wasn't enough. He needed to get them both somewhere warm right now.

That left one option.

"There's a fire lookout a few miles north of here, which is closer than the house at this point," he said. "It's not really used anymore, but last time I stopped by, there was a communication center that still worked. There should also be some food and water they keep in storage for emergencies."

"So we could call for help?"

Griffin nodded. "Once the weather dies down, they could bring in a helicopter to pick us up. That would be the quickest way in and out at this point."

He started to turn the snowmobile around but the motor sputtered and died.

No… This couldn't be happening.

The wind whipped through his clothes as he quickly evaluated the situation. He knew all too well the dangers of exposure in this weather. Even dressed in layers, they were both at risk for frostbite or hypothermia if he didn't get them somewhere safe quickly. He was already questioning his decision to take her to the watchtower and not back to the ranch, but in this weather, he'd believed that the quicker he could get her somewhere safe, the better. And with Jinx headed this way, he wasn't sure he had a choice.

He yanked the pull start, praying the machine would come to life.

Nothing.

His heart pounded as he jumped onto the side of the snowmobile. He had no idea how long he had before the men would manage to get loose, or when his rescue backup would arrive. No. He had to get Tory out if he intended to keep her safe.

"What's wrong with it?" she shouted above the wind.

"The temperatures are too cold. It's having trouble starting again."

He turned on the choke to start…twisted the key. Nothing. He gave it some gas and the engine finally caught. Griffin blew a sigh of relief into the cold night air.

"Hang on."

He backtracked for about a mile then headed west toward the tower. He'd told her the truth about the last time he'd been there, but that had been two summers ago, and the place had probably been neglected since then. While it had been a favorite place of theirs growing up, he was pretty sure his brothers and the ranch hands didn't get out there very often anymore.

Memories of him and his brothers surfaced. They'd camped out in the tower more than once, roasting marshmallows in a firepit below, and waking up to see the sunrise. Even as a boy, he'd appreciated the golden glow covering miles and miles of forested land.

So much had changed over the past decade, but they'd managed to maintain the same sense of closeness and family. And things would continue to change. Liam was married, and Griffin had no doubt more spouses and grandchildren would follow in the coming years.

As for him, why did he feel so…stuck?

He kept his eyes on the path for any fallen trees or debris, worried there might not be food or a way to communicate after all this time. But he could only worry about one thing at a time. At least the place would have shelter, and he was certain it had a pile of blankets. They'd be fine for now.

Within fifteen minutes, just as he could no longer feel his fingers or his toes, the tower finally came into view, barely visible in the moonlight. He parked the snowmobile behind a large crop of bushes, thinking that with the snow covering their tracks, they should be able to stay hidden.

He jumped off then helped Tory. "You okay?"

"Yeah…" She shivered next to him. "Just cold."

He grabbed her hand and hurried her toward the two-story structure that stood at least seventy feet off the ground on the top of a ridge. On any other day, he would have loved watching the sunrise with her. But today…

Today he just needed to make sure he kept her alive.

EIGHT

Tory climbed the steep, narrow stairs up the side of the watchtower and then stomped off the snow before stepping into the small building. Inside wasn't warm, but at least the structure blocked the wind.

Griffin clicked on a flashlight, revealing the sparsely furnished room that held a bed, a table and chairs, and a couple of supply cabinets, all surrounded by four walls of windows. She glanced around the room with its three-hundred-and-sixty-degree view still shaded in darkness and tried to imagine the incredible sight once the sun came up. There was no doubt the scenery was breathtaking.

She stopped in the middle of the room where a round wooden table encased a large circular map.

"Do you know what this is?" Griffin asked.

"To state the obvious, a map."

"Yes, but this is an original Osborne Firefinder from the 1930s."

She ran her finger across the smooth top, her curiosity piqued. "What does it do?"

"It was used to find the exact location of a fire—even

in the dark. Basically, it's a topographic map with two sighting apertures that can be moved so that the fire is aligned in the crosshairs and its location determined. It's not used anymore, but my father always loved it, and really, it's a piece of history. The original version was invented back in 1840 by Sir Francis Ronalds in the UK."

"Wow…there is a lot of history up here." She glanced back at the windows. "And I can't wait to see the view once the sun rises."

"We need to arrange it so you're up here on a clear day, because you're right—" he walked over to where she was standing "—the views are spectacular. You can see for miles from up here."

"I'd love that."

And she would. Except she had no plans of staying that long. She knew he was trying to distract her from the reality of the situation, but all she wanted was for this to be over. Even if that meant walking away from the intriguing man standing next to her.

He clicked off the flashlight. "We have to keep any extra light to a minimum. Thankfully, the snow's tapered off and there's some moonlight."

"I need the flashlight for one thing." She pulled off the scarf around her neck and looked up at him. "Take off your coat, so I can check out your rib cage. I want to see how much damage they did."

"I'm fine, Tory—"

"You're not fine." She waited for him to comply then stepped in front of him and laid her hands against his rib cage. "Take a deep breath for me."

"Tory…"

She ignored his stubbornness and focused on listening to his breathing. She needed a stethoscope and, even more important, needed to get him to a hospital. But for now, aside from making sure a broken rib hadn't punctured a lung, there wasn't really anything she could do.

"Lung function doesn't seem compromised," she said, pulling up the bottom of his shirt, "but there is bruising on the skin, which is a sign for bruised or broken ribs. Without an X-ray, though, there is no way to know the exact damage done. Any shortness of breath?"

"No."

"What about when you take a breath. Any pain?"

"Nothing I can't manage."

"It's important you keep the pain under control, because if you don't breathe deeply because of it, you could develop pneumonia." She looked up at him and realized her hand was still on his chest. She quickly pulled away and took a step back. "Any other pain?"

"Besides the gunshot wound?"

She squirmed beneath his piercing gaze as she checked the wound for signs of infection with help from the flashlight. "It's looking okay for now, but I can't help but wonder if this is the norm and you're always a magnet for trouble."

He shot her a wide grin. "From what I've seen so far today, I'm not the only one."

She couldn't help but laugh as she started opening cupboard doors until she found a first-aid kit. "I'm giving you some paracetamol, then I'll change your bandage."

"Yes, ma'am."

"You need to make sure you keep your lungs clear, which means you also shouldn't sleep lying down. And you have to walk around every hour or so. Just until we're able to get you to a hospital."

"I have to say, I think being stranded with you gives me the advantage."

Her heart fluttered and she realized she was interpreting what he was saying all wrong. He wasn't interested in her. He was simply thankful for her medical knowledge.

"This is serious," she said, focusing on her task, "but the good thing is that even if one is broken, normally ribs are left to heal naturally because they can't be splinted. You just need to watch for worsening pain, shortness of breath or fever."

Tory was trying not to worry about him, but while the majority of her memories were still suppressed, she knew the risks of a chest infection and the possibility that a broken rib could puncture something. But she wasn't going to let her mind go there. He had to be okay.

She moved to a window and stared out into the darkness, praying it would hide them from Jinx and the others until rescue came. "How high do you think we are on this ridge?"

"Over ten thousand feet—plus the stairs we just climbed."

"That would explain why I'm out of breath."

"The altitude is hard on some people who aren't used to it. Why don't you take a quick inventory of what's here, like food, bedding and candles? I still don't have any cell signal, but I'll see if I can get the radio working. And while there isn't any running water, there should be some containers of water."

"I'll see what I can find."

She started through the cabinets one at a time. Supplies were definitely limited, but there was fuel for the propane lights, matches and a small stash of food and blankets. Enough to keep them warm and fed if they ended up being stuck for more than a few hours.

Static buzzed from the radio for a few seconds before a voice crackled over the line.

"Griffin? Griffin, is that you?"

"Becket." Griffin blew out a sharp breath of relief at the deputy's voice. "It is, and I can't tell you how glad I am to hear your voice. We're at the fire lookout tower north of my parents' ranch."

"We heard they grabbed you at the house."

"They did, but we managed to escape. What about my parents? Are they okay?"

"They're shook up and worried about you, but they're fine. They're going to be glad to hear from you. What about the two of you? Are you both okay?"

"Let's just say it's a good thing we managed to get out of there when we did, but we need a helicopter extraction as soon as the sun comes up."

"We've got the weather to contend with, but the forecast is predicting that the storm will start dying out by morning. As long as the winds stay down, we should be able to evacuate you. What do you know about the men who grabbed you?"

"There were two of them, and they're intent on finding Tory. But Jinx is on his way, and I'm sure he'll be armed and with backup. According to the men who took us, he'll be coming in from the north edge of the property on the trail that leads south."

"Is there any way they could follow you to your current location?"

"It's possible, which means you have to plan to come with backup. They've hired one of my father's old ranch hands, which gives them the advantage of knowing the layout of the ranch, but I'm counting on you to get us out of here before they have a chance to show up."

"Copy that. We'll be prepared with extra deputies just in case. I'll give you an update on our ETA as soon as we're able to take off."

"Appreciate it."

"Stay safe."

Tory stepped up beside him. "So first thing in the morning they'll be here?"

"As long as the weather clears."

She bit the edge of her lip, trying not to worry about what would happen if the men managed to track them down and find them first. But not worrying felt impossible.

"How much ammunition do we have?" she asked.

"Not enough to fight our way out of here, but a few defensive shots are better than nothing."

She nodded, knowing she had to trust them to get her out. Thankful she wasn't trying to do this alone.

"My suggestion is that we get a couple hours of sleep before the sun comes up," he said, standing. "I think we'll both feel better then. There are two beds here we can use. I can guarantee they're not the most comfortable beds you've ever slept in but—"

"Trust me, a bed sounds good no matter how bad it is at this point."

He let out a low laugh. "Agreed."

She started toward the other side of the room, accidently brushing her leg against the table. She winced at the stab of pain that radiated up her leg.

"What's wrong?"

She glanced down at the sore spot. Her sweats were ripped at the site. "It's probably just a scratch."

"Let me look."

She frowned. "You're the one I'm worried about. The one who at the least has a bruised rib and your left eye has already turned half a dozen colors since we left. I think a scratch—"

He shot her an insistent grin. "Stop playing stubborn like me and let me look."

"Fine." She pulled up the pant leg with the rip and caught sight of a six-inch cut that had already started turning red. She had no idea how she'd missed it, but all she needed was an antibiotic cream and she'd be good to go.

"It really is just a scratch."

"It's not just a scratch. It must have happened on the snowmobile. You're going to need a tetanus shot after this."

"Thanks for the diagnosis, Dr. O'Callaghan." She shot him a grin. "We make quite a pair, don't we?"

"We sure do." He grabbed the first-aid kit she'd just used on him, turned and caught her gaze. "I'll get you patched up, then we're both going to bed. I have a feeling tomorrow will be an exhausting day."

An hour later Tory jerked awake. Perspiration beaded across her forehead, even though there was a chill in the room. Shadows played against the wall as she fought to remember where she was. Reality flooded through her like a tidal wave as the wind whipped against the windows of the fire tower.

She'd been dreaming she was trying to save someone from a burning car. But who? Could it be the person who had gone hiking with her that day? Or maybe someone else she was close to who could get hurt if they were dragged into this mess? What she couldn't remember was any details. Only that she needed to save someone. She searched her memory for a name, but came up blank. She sat up in the bed, frustration eating at her.

"Tory, are you okay?"

Griffin stood in the doorway, a shadow in the room only lit by a stream of moonlight filtering through the windows.

"I'm sorry if I woke you."

"I was up, but you screamed then kept mumbling something I couldn't understand."

"It was nothing. Just a bad dream."

"Do you want to tell me about it?"

She didn't want to go there again, but maybe retelling the dream would help bring clarity. Her mind was trying to recall something.

"I was back at the crash scene. The agents were dead on the ground, but I wasn't in the car this time. I was trying to save someone else who was inside the car."

"Do you know who?"

She tried to pull up the memory. Had she seen the victim's face? A blurred image surfaced. It had been a woman, but it wasn't anyone she knew. Or was it?

Elizabeth.

The name shot to the surface, bringing with it a trickle of memories.

"Elizabeth." Her gaze snapped to his. "It was my sister in that car."

"Wait a minute…" Griffin sat beside her on the edge of the bed. "According to the FBI report, you don't have a sister. You're an only child."

"I know, but we already know there is a leak. Maybe the agents already knew that. There was no mention of a second witness at the murder scene, and no mention of my sister, but I remember her. All of this has to tie together somehow."

"You think she might be the second witness."

"I'm still not sure, but it's possible. Or it could just be my subconscious warning me there is someone else Jinx can use against me."

Someone had divulged the route her escort had taken, a move that had almost cost Tory her life and had taken the lives of two agents. If the FBI had believed there could be a mole, they might have taken measures to protect her, her family and whoever else was involved by purposely leaving names out of the file and any written communication.

"Okay." He stood and started pacing in front of her as his mind ran through the implications. "Can you remember anything about your sister?"

Tory nodded. "Her name's Elizabeth Joy. She's twenty-two years old and just graduated from university."

"And in your dream, you needed to protect her." He stopped in front of her and caught her gaze. "Just like in real life. Do you remember her being there with you the day of the murders?" he asked.

Tory let out a sharp breath. "I'm trying, but no. I still can't recall anything about that day."

At least the memories were beginning to appear. That was a start.

"I must have wanted to ensure there was no paper trail of her existence," Tory continued. "No family that Jinx could go after. That makes total sense. I'm a witness to a high-profile murder case. Family could mean leverage if they got hold of them."

He blew out a sharp huff. There was still something brothering him. "It's hard to imagine them not being able to connect the two of you. In the world of social media, completely erasing a connection with someone is almost impossible. Leaving your sister off an FBI report is one thing, but erasing the online footprint? I'm not sure that would be possible."

Tory shrugged. "I can't answer that. How much time do you spend on social media?"

"Pretty much none, but I'm the exception. Not the rule."

"Maybe I'm the same, though I can't be sure at this point. What's bothering me right now is the struggle to discern what is real from the files, my own blurred memories and now my dreams. Elizabeth seems so real, but what if my mind is somehow twisting things? Making people up to fill in the blanks in my memory."

"What does your gut say?" he asked.

"She's real."

"Then let's go with that for now. Do you have any other memories of her?"

Tory closed her eyes for a moment. "I have a few, but things are still fuzzy. Her twenty-second birthday…her cat…going to the beach last summer…graduation…"

"That's a great start. You're accessing your memories. It seems to me that it will only be a matter of time before they all come back."

"I hope so."

He tried to build a scenario from what they had so far. Tory and Elizabeth had gone on vacation…two sisters enjoying hiking in Colorado together. But it also could have been a friend or someone she knew from work. At this point they couldn't be completely sure about anything. What they did know was that she hadn't been alone that day. She'd been hiking with another woman, possibly her sister. Hopefully her memories would tell them the truth.

"I still think my mom's advice was the best," he said. "Don't try to dredge up the memories. Just let them come naturally. And they will come."

He moved too quickly to turn on the kettle and winced at the pain.

Tory noticed. "I'm worried about you. What's your pain level on a scale of one to ten?"

"A three…maybe a four. But I did take some pain medicine earlier, so it has to be helping."

She stopped next to him. "All of this…it's something that happens in some suspense thriller, not to someone like me. I work in a hospital and, from what I've managed to put together, I live a pretty ordinary life. I hang out with friends, go to work and church, but escaping on a snowmobile from a couple criminals? I can promise you that wasn't on my agenda this week."

He caught the pain in her voice. All it had taken was being in the wrong place at the wrong time and everything in her life had changed. And more than likely nothing in her life would be the same again.

"I'll be honest, I'm terrified, Griffin. On TV, someone can get shot half a dozen times in the chest and still save the world. I work the reality end in the emergency room and that doesn't happen. People die."

He nodded, but he had no unreasonable expectations about saving the world.

He just wanted to save her.

He tried to shake off the unexpected wave of emotion and glanced out the window. The snow had finally stopped and the clouds had parted enough to leave a trail of moonlight on the snow. It wouldn't be long until the sun started to rise and, he hoped, their rescue arrived.

"I have a feeling neither of us is going to get any more sleep. I know I could use some coffee. I'll put on the kettle, but I also want to show you something."

He filled the kettle with water, put it on the gas then led her out onto the catwalk that surrounded the upper floor. The wind whipping around them was icy, but the moonlit view of the snow-covered terrain below was worth it.

"What do you think?" he asked.

"Wow. I feel like I just stepped into a painting. This is so beautiful."

Strange how he'd suddenly felt this overwhelming urge to share with her a part of his world. And the mountains were a part of who he was. This land was a part of him.

"There's nothing like watching a sunrise or sunset over the mountains, but seeing it by moonlight is like standing in the middle of a winter wonderland."

"If I lived here, I'd never get anything done. I think I'd simply stare out the windows all day long."

He laughed, enjoying her enthusiasm. "And the view changes every season. Wildflowers in the spring...the explosion of colors in the fall... The scenery never gets old to me."

He looked up at the sky. "And on a clear night you can see the Milky Way...maybe a meteor shower and a planet or two."

"Wildflowers in the spring." She shoved her hands into the coat pockets and turned to him. "I remember having this conversation with my sister. She loved aspen daisies and the mountains, and we visited the area together a few times."

"You remember hiking that day?"

"Not specifically...it's still just fragments. I'm not sure whether Elizabeth was in Colorado with me for that trip. She'd just graduated from college, and I remember her being very focused on job searching. She had a summer internship she hoped would lead to something more permanent." She glanced up at him. "I guess you've never considered leaving this place."

He hesitated at the sudden change of subject. "Sometimes. I mean...as much as I love the mountains, sometimes I wonder if there's more out there."

"What do you mean?"

She was shivering in the cold beside him. He needed to get her inside.

"Your cheeks are flushed. We should move out of the cold."

He put his hand on her elbow and hurried her back inside, wanting to ignore her question. The water in the kettle was just starting to simmer. He pulled out a couple of mugs, thankful for the distraction.

"I'm sorry…" She grabbed the jars of instant coffee and sugar. "I didn't mean to get too personal."

"It's fine. I've just never talked about leaving— especially with my family, who wouldn't understand." He hesitated again, wondering why he was even considering telling her. "But I have been toying with the idea of leaving Timber Falls for quite some time."

"Really?" She stopped in front of him. "I'm surprised. Especially because all your family is here."

"It's not that I don't love my family." He started scooping the coffee and sugar into the mugs. "In fact, it doesn't have anything to do with them, really."

"Then why leave? You seem to have such a fulfilling life. A family who cares about you, a great job and a stunning ranch with incredible views…"

But no one to share it with.

He shoved away the thought. He'd dated a handful of women. Even tried his hand at online dating thanks to the insistence of his brothers, but that had been a waste of time. None of the women he'd gone out with had clicked. He drew in a sharp breath. If he were honest with himself, that wasn't the real reason he'd avoided a serious relationship for so long.

"You're right," he said, "but do you ever feel that way? Like something seems…missing?"

"You mean someone?"

"Maybe." He had no intention of admitting to her what he was really thinking.

"It's funny." She shrugged. "I feel like I would *know* if there's someone in my life. But if there is, I still can't pull up those memories."

The kettle started to whistle. He pulled it off the stove and filled up their mugs.

"I'll admit I'm surprised you're not married or have a girlfriend," she said. "Sharing your life with someone— wherever you might be—would be nice."

The candle he'd lit earlier flickered at the edge of the room as he set the mugs on the small table. She'd managed to underscore what he'd been thinking and he couldn't deny it was true. After watching his younger brother fall in love, he'd seen something in their relationship that he wanted. Just like the relationship his parents had. But maybe Tory was right. Maybe finding fulfillment didn't have anything to do with where you were but rather who you were with. And, for some reason, being with her had reminded him of something he longed for.

It had also reminded him of everything he'd lost. And going there again terrified him.

Tory sat beside him then shifted her attention to the window. "Did you hear that?"

He nodded. A distinct knocking noise was coming from outside. He unholstered his gun and quickly blew out the candle.

"Stay in here, away from the windows. I'll be back."

Someone was out there.

NINE

Tory heard another sharp rapping noise as she watched Griffin step out onto the catwalk. The icy wind rushed through the room before he shut the door behind him. If Jinx and his men were out there, she and Griffin were completely defenseless except for a few rounds from the guns he'd confiscated from them. And as competent he was as a deputy, that didn't change the fact that they were outnumbered and outgunned.

God is our refuge...a very present help in trouble. Therefore we will not fear...

The words from Psalm came to mind automatically, but how was she supposed to let go of fear when someone wanted to silence her. How could she deal with everything that had happened?

She glanced around the darkened room then reached for a walking stick she'd seen earlier. Moonlight danced across the floor as clouds rolled past. She wasn't going to let Griffin try to defend them on his own. There had to be a way to defeat the men. Together.

The wind took her breath away as she stepped onto the catwalk. She pressed her body against the window and listened for voices, but all she could hear was the wind howling against the structure.

Where was Griffin?

She started toward the staircase. If Jinx thought she was here, there was only one way up. She wished they had a plan. One that would give them the advantage with the element of surprise, but was that even possible with their limited options?

She heard a noise behind her and turned around, the stick raised above her head.

"Whoa… Tory…" Griffin stepped from the shadows. "What are you doing out here?"

"I'm sorry, but I was worried and didn't want leave you out here on your own."

"You're going to make me worry if you don't stay out of the potential line of fire."

"You've already taken enough risks for me. I won't let that happen again."

"No risk, they're not here." He holstered his weapon. "Looks like it was just a loose tile on the roof, flapping in the wind."

She breathed a sigh of relief at his response and glanced over the edge of the snow-covered railing. A hint of moonlight had emerged from behind the clouds, leaving a white glow. But this time she couldn't see the beauty of the surrounding view. Jinx and his men might not be here yet, but they were out there and determined to find her.

Griffin wiped a snowflake off her cheek. "We're going to get through this. I promise."

But he couldn't promise her that. No matter how

much he wanted to protect her, there were limits to what he could do at this point.

"And if they show up?" She raised her walking stick. "How are we supposed to defend against them?"

"We have the advantage of being up here."

She frowned. While it was true that they might have a better line of sight from their position, she wasn't convinced this was any safer. She still felt completely vulnerable.

"Let's get back inside where it's warm," he said. "The sun will be up in an hour, which means this is almost over."

So that was it. They just had to make it another hour.

The wind caught the door as he opened it, slamming it wide. A second later a pile of snow slid off the roof and dumped onto Griffin's head. He let out a shout then quickly shook it off before stepping into the room.

She couldn't help but giggle as she followed him inside, scurrying to light the candle and find him a blanket.

"You think it's funny?" he asked.

"Oh, it's definitely funny."

He grabbed a clump of snow stuck to his jacket shoulder and threw it at her, catching her by surprise.

"I was going to tell you that I owe you one, but we might be even now." She realized how tired he looked despite the mischievous smile on his lips. "You never went to sleep, did you?"

He shook his head like it was no big deal. "Sleep is overrated."

"Says who? You look exhausted."

"There is no way I could sleep now. Besides, you told me not to lay down."

"I never meant you shouldn't sleep." She lit the candle and then grabbed her cup off the table, needing a distraction from his nearness. "How about a refill? I'm sure these are cold."

"I'd like that." He turned on the gas stove again for the kettle. "Have you been able to remember anything else about your sister?"

"A few things, but it's strange how the memories surface. At first there are random pieces, but every time I think something comes together, I find another hole."

"So you still don't remember who was with you that day?"

Tory shook her head. "When I think about it, I feel as if I'm protecting someone. But I can't see their face. It makes sense that Elizabeth was the one with me that day, but I can't ever quite see what happened. It's scary."

"It will come. I'm sure of it."

"But when and at what price? And there's something else that scares me. Someone in the FBI had to know there was another witness, assuming I told them. It makes sense that I might have tried to make a deal to protect whoever was with me. Especially if it was Elizabeth."

"I know this has been hard, Tory, but I was given the job to protect you, and I plan to do just that."

She caught his gaze, surprised by the intensity of his expression. She felt her heart pound. There was something about his eyes that managed to pierce straight through her, and for a moment, she wanted him to do more than just protect her. She wanted him to gather her into his arms and kiss her…

But no. She wasn't under any false illusions. His motivation to protect her stemmed from his job. From a sense of duty. Nothing more. And it was crazy to think there was anything personal about the situation. Besides, she certainly wasn't in a position to allow her own feelings to get carried away. Not when she was still struggling to pull up memories of who she was.

"Let's try another angle," he said. "What do you remember about your hometown?"

His question yanked her back to reality.

She closed her eyes and worked to pull the pieces together. "Adobe houses…snow in the winter…green chile stew."

"Green chile stew?" He scrunched his brows together. "Arizona… New Mexico?"

Something clicked in her mind. "Santa Fe."

"Now that's progress. I visited there once. It's beautiful."

"It is. The Rocky Mountains, large plains, and a rich history…" Details continued to emerge, but nothing about that day. Why couldn't she remember?

"I have an apartment in the city close to where I work, but I've always loved coming up here on vacation. Even dreamed about having my own cabin up here one day."

She breathed in, relieved at the memories that were emerging. Terrified of the ones she still couldn't grasp.

"I have a piece of land I bought a few years ago," Griffin said. "You'd love it. There are views of the mountains, lots of pines and aspens, hunting, fishing…"

His pause left space for her to imagine briefly the two of them building a home and raising a family. She pushed away the thoughts. That wasn't a place she needed to go to. His job—his only job—was to keep her safe. Nothing more.

"You mentioned you'd thought of leaving here," she said. "What are you looking for?"

"Funny…my brother just asked me the same thing."

"What did you tell him?"

"That I didn't know," he said.

"Sometimes it's not the place that matters most, but rather the person you're with."

"That's pretty profound."

She yawned as the kettle started whistling again and she moved to fill their mugs, not sure why she'd said that. Was there someone back home waiting for her? Someone she was already planning to put down roots with?

She yawned again then handed him his drink, unable to shake both the fatigue and the fear.

"Why don't you go lie down another hour until the sun comes up?" he said. "You'll feel better."

"There's no way I can sleep. The bad weather didn't stop Jinx's men before, and I know it won't stop them now." She glanced at the dark windows and tried to stuff down the looming fear. "Lately, I've wondered which is more frightening. Reality or my dreams. I can't escape it."

"Fear can be debilitating." Griffin took a sip of his coffee. "I was at a men's breakfast a couple of weeks ago with my church. They were discussing when Jesus was out on the boat with his disciples during the storm, and how fear is tied to doubt. It reminded me that no matter what is happening around me, God is in control. It almost sounds like a cliché, but He told us not to be afraid or discouraged because He is with us."

She knew he was right, but that still didn't make it easy. "It's hard when there's a storm raging out there both literally and figuratively. I believe God's in control. But this...? I don't know how to handle all of this."

"And I don't think Jesus was saying we couldn't fear. Fears in this world are real. Think about how Elijah feared Jezebel, Moses feared facing Pharaoh and the Israelites, Elijah was depressed. But God was always with them. Even through the tough moments."

"Then why is putting that into practice so hard?" she asked.

"You have to believe He's still there. Every step of the way."

When you go through the deep waters, I will be with you.

She liked Griffin because he wasn't afraid to voice his weaknesses or to admit he relied on someone else. There seemed to be something refreshing about that.

"I needed that reminder, because all of this...it's pretty overwhelming for me." She took a sip of her drink. "Can I ask you something personal?"

"Okay."

"When I asked you earlier if you'd ever been afraid for your life or for someone you loved, you told me about a situation with your brother and his wife. But I sensed there was someone else you were thinking about."

She set down her coffee, suddenly feeling the tension that had slipped between them. She had no idea why she'd felt the urge to ask him such a probing question, except she'd seen something in his eyes that had left her wondering what he hadn't told her. And now that same look of sadness was back.

Griffin shifted in his chair at the question. This loss wasn't something he talked about. Not even to his family. Too much hurt came with the memories, so leaving it in the past had always seemed like the best thing to do. But something about this situation and Tory sitting beside him made him want to peel back the thick layers of protection around his heart and share with her on a deeper level.

"Her name was Lilly," he began. "We met at university and started dating our sophomore year. I eventually met her family, and was thinking about proposing, but there was something she didn't really talk to me about until it was too late."

The howling wind whipped around the structure as the memories began to emerge. He drew in a slow breath while Tory sat silent beside him, waiting for him to continue. Part of him wanted to find an excuse to change the subject. The other part wanted her to understand him more.

"She had an old boyfriend," he said, finally continuing. "Parker Reynolds. They dated throughout high school, but then she broke up with him the summer after they graduated. He stayed in their small hometown and worked while she left for college, but he was obsessed with her and resented the breakup. Couldn't stand the idea that she didn't love him and was going out with other guys while she was away from home.

"At first, he just sent text messages or left voice mails, but then he started physically stalking her. He'd show up at her job or apartment and leave some clue that he'd been there, or talk to someone she knew, asking questions and creeping them out."

"And she never told you any of this?"

He shook his head. "She did mention there was this crazy guy who she'd gone out with in high school, but she made me think it wasn't a big deal. Like, he was just an old boyfriend. I never thought he'd hurt her. And I don't think she did, either."

"I can't even imagine."

"The day she went missing, we were supposed to meet for dinner, but I ended up canceling at the last minute because I had a big paper due and needed to work. She said that was fine, but that she needed to talk to me about something later that night. I probably wouldn't have worried too much, except she normally would have answered when I called and I couldn't get hold of her. I thought she'd gone to bed early."

But that wasn't why she hadn't answered.

"The next morning my phone rang. I expected it to be her, but it wasn't. Instead it was her parents and I knew at that moment something horrible had happened."

And it had.

He stood and went to the window, wishing he could erase the guilt. He'd dealt with it over the years the best he could, sticking it into a box and trying to stuff it away, but all these years later the guilt over not stopping what happened to Lilly was still there when he thought about her.

"The police had found her body in the trunk of a car."

Tory pressed her hand against her mouth. "Oh, Griffin... I am so, so sorry. I can't even imagine how hard that had to have been to go through. How much something like that must still affect you today."

He felt the familiar guilt well up as she stared at the flickering candle casting shadows across the room. "If I'd been with her that evening like I'd promised... If I hadn't let work get in the way...she might be alive today. I'll never know, but I believe she wanted to tell me about him. Instead she died and I..."

He tried to swallow the lump in his throat.

"Couldn't save her," she finally finished for him.

Griffin nodded.

"It wasn't your fault."

"That's what everyone told me, but it's still hard not to ask the what-if."

"Is that why you became a deputy?"

He caught her gaze, amazed at how she seemed able to read him. To understand him.

"At the time I was studying sports medicine, but after that...it changed me. I knew I couldn't sit back and let something like that happen to someone else."

"So you're atoning for the guilt."

"I didn't say that."

"But you were thinking it. And I think you still believe you have to. Think about why you're sitting here right now. You didn't have to agree to the FBI's request. You could have easily passed me off to someone else, but you didn't."

He didn't want to admit it, but somehow she'd managed to hit the truth straight on.

"Do you know what I see?" she continued.

He shook his head, not sure he wanted to hear what she had to say.

"I see a man with a love for family and country. A man who would do anything to help someone else. A man who would put his life on the line to save not only the woman he loves, like with Lilly, but a complete stranger like me. Losing Lilly is now a part of who you are, and that can never be changed."

Griffin turned away from her probing gaze. He hadn't intended to open up to her, but there was something more going on here than just protecting an assigned case. He wanted to keep her safe, but he also couldn't shake the feelings that were growing. He couldn't go there again, though. Besides, he'd dated a few women over the years since Lilly's death, but no one had ever been able to break down the wall around his heart, and he had no intention of changing that now.

And that wasn't the only issue. How well could he get to know Tory when she didn't remember who she was? He'd somehow managed to make this job personal, something he never should have done. It was his duty to save and protect her. And when this was over, he'd move on. Nothing more would come of this.

"I'm sorry if I pushed," she said.

"Forget it."

He dumped the rest of his now cold coffee in the sink. He'd explained to Tory how losing someone he loved had changed him and made him who he was today. That didn't mean he was interested in her romantically, and even if he was, she would leave when all this was over. He started rinsing out the cup. It was time to get his personal feelings out of the way.

"Griffin?"

He glanced across the room to where she still sat.

"Do you smell smoke?"

Griffin ran toward the window of the watchtower, praying she was just being paranoid, but he smelled something, as well. Still, a forest fire this time of year with the terrain covered in snow was highly unlikely.

Unless it wasn't an accident.

"Yeah…I smell it, too."

He followed the window around then discovered the source of the smoke. Yellow and orange flames crackled along the bottom of the tower as the strong scent of gasoline mingled with the burning timber above the bottom floor's stone foundation. The muscles in his jaw tensed. They were here. Jinx's men. This was definitely no accident. They'd set the structure on fire.

TEN

"Griffin, how are we supposed to get out of here?"

He caught the panic in Tory's voice as he quickly ran through their options. Even if it were possible to put out the fire, there was no running water in the facility, but that wasn't their biggest issue at the moment. There was only one exit, which meant that to get out they had to go outside and take the stairs. No doubt Jinx's men would be waiting for them at the bottom, leaving them vulnerable to an ambush, which he was sure was their plan. He felt for his gun, still in his holster, worried about the consequences of a showdown. If they tried to escape down those stairs, one or both of them was liable to get shot, because Jinx wasn't going to play games. He was here to get the information he needed to end this.

"Griffin?"

He turned to her, glad to catch the spark of determination in her eye. She was ready to fight, which was exactly what they needed, but she was also relying on him to get them out of this.

"We have to find a way to use the fire against them."

Grabbing one of the flashlights and turning it on, he started rummaging through the cabinets where the supplies were kept, still formulating his plan. If the men were expecting them to escape down the stairwell, they had to do the unexpected. But they had to hurry.

"The smoke," she said. "We could use it for cover."

He nodded. "That's what I'm thinking. See if you can find something to cover our faces."

He stopped for a moment and glanced out the windows again to determine the direction of the wind. The smoke was blowing north, which was perfect for his plan. He dug through the cabinet where they'd found the first-aid kit, water, flashlights and other supplies.

"What are you looking for?"

"There used to be some rope in here." He opened the last cupboard and finally found what he was looking for. He quickly pulled out the large coils sitting in the back of one of the cupboards. "Do you know anything about rappelling?"

She handed him a dishcloth for his face and frowned. "You mean rappelling with just a rope? No harness or anchor?"

He nodded. "I know it's risky, but they're waiting for us below. If we walk down those stairs, there will be no way out of this. We've got to find an advantage."

This time it was fear that registered in her eyes. "You're wanting to rappel down the backside of the structure?"

He nodded again. "I know it sounds crazy, but the smoke should hide our movements if we hurry and they're not expecting us to climb down."

"I agree, but what about you? You're in no condition to rappel out of here. If you have a broken rib, you could easily puncture a lung by putting too much strain on your rib cage."

"I'm aware of the risks, but I think this is the only way."

She glanced again toward the door then nodded. "Let's do it."

He could hear voices below getting louder. There was no way to know how many men were out there, but he couldn't worry about that right now. He knew they'd taken their positions and were waiting for the opportunity to pounce.

He started praying. Not only that the wind didn't change, but that he'd be able to physically make it. He didn't want Tory to know his level of pain. But he'd find a way to push through. He had no choice. And they had to hurry. If they didn't escape soon, he had a feeling the men would come for them.

"So you have done this before?" he asked.

"Set an anchor, wrap the rope and start your descent. I can do that."

He was surprised at her response, but also relieved. Rappelling without the necessary equipment, though doable, was dangerous. And, for the moment, their one chance out of here.

"There's no time to update the sheriff's office, but the sun will be up soon. If they're not on their way now, they should be soon."

"And if Jinx and his men try to come up here?" she asked.

"Then I'll have to make every shot count, but I'm hoping to avoid a showdown."

Griffin signaled for her to tie the towels around her face. Beyond what they were doing now, all he could do was pray that the winds had died down enough to make a helicopter extraction possible. In the meantime, they had to do this on their own.

The smoke continued to thicken as they made their way to the back of the first story. He could hear the flames crackling, lapping at the thick wooden beams his grandfather had erected a century ago. His body ached as he found the best spot on the catwalk to make a descent. They worked quickly together on the catwalks to set the anchor by looping the rope around two thick poles that were strong enough to hold them. He monitored Tory's progress while they worked, pleased at how quickly she followed his lead. She must have been doing more than just hiking the day she'd witnessed the murders. She clearly had experience with rappelling and climbing, which was going to make what they were about to do a whole lot easier.

A minute later they dropped the ends of their ropes and let them fall to the ground. He could hear the men shouting below them on the other side of the tower, but there was no way to know if their plan had been discovered.

She followed his lead as he pulled his rope around his hip, over his shoulder then back down his arm. The friction of the rope against his body would slow his descent and stop a fall. They'd have to control the rate of descent by monitoring how fast the rope passed through their hands.

"Make sure you don't let go of the rope," he said.

"Don't worry. I have no intention of doing that."

They climbed over the railing and each began scaling a structural beam. He ignored the piercing jab in his side that seemed to grow with each step, and worked instead to ensure that most of the pressure was on his good arm. He prayed she was wrong about his ribs, but this was a risk he'd have to take. While the men might still need Tory alive, he knew he was completely disposable.

He glanced down at the halfway point. They were still probably at least fifty or sixty feet above the ground, but all they had to do was get off the structure without being followed, then make it to that helo he prayed was on its way. The heat of the fire intensified around them. At some point the structure would collapse. They just had to make it to the bottom before that happened.

Griffin brushed away the wave of emotion that hit. His grandfather had overseen the building of the tower in the early 1900s and it had stood for all this time. But he couldn't worry about what would be lost. All he had to focus on was getting Tory out of there alive.

Tory could hear men's voices behind them as she edged her way down the large support beam. Somehow the feel of the rope in her hand and the descent seemed familiar, but that didn't take away the terror flooding her chest. She couldn't dwell on that. Instead she fought to focus on one step at a time. That's all they could do while praying that they managed to find a way out alive.

Her lungs fought for air as she glanced at Griffin. His mouth and nose were covered with the dishcloth to block the smoke, but she could still see the intensity in his eyes. He was in pain. What scared her the most was that if Jinx and his men found them, they wouldn't just beat him. This time they'd find a way to get the information they wanted, then kill him.

Her gaze shifted up as she tried to pinpoint the location of the men. Shouts came from behind them, but she couldn't see them. Her legs threatened to collapse as she hit the ground. She shot out a sharp breath of relief and started pulling off her rope. They were running out of time. They had seconds at the most until the men discovered where they were.

"You good?" Griffin asked.

She nodded. Her legs were shaking, but she had no intention of letting that slow her down. "We need to get out of here."

She felt her heart pound as she dropped the rope onto the ground. Griffin had been right. Their escape down the back of the tower had given them the advantage of surprise, but once the men recognized what they'd done, they'd be seconds behind.

Griffin grabbed her hand and started pulling her toward the tree line. It was still snowing, but not as heavy as it had been during the night. Still, the recent snowfall had added up to at least half a foot of additional coverage and the drifts were even deeper. Icy cold wind bore through her coat and gloves, leaving her lungs burning with every breath.

She could hear Griffin's labored breathing as he ran beside her, partly from the cold, she was sure, but also from the fact that he'd taken a beating to his rib cage. Adrenaline was probably masking most of the pain, but not all of it. And there was no time for her to stop to check out just how much damage there was. They had to keep moving.

Someone on the catwalk shouted.

Tory looked back to see someone standing in a haze of smoke. The fire had started to abate and the men must have just realized that they'd climbed down.

A bullet smashed into a tree behind them, sending another rush of adrenaline through her. Griffin ran his arm around her waist, helping to pick up her speed. Every step felt like her feet were made of lead and her pant leg rubbed against the cut on her leg. She willed her mind to block out the distractions. They just needed to keep running.

Keep running.

That's all she could think about. One step in front of another. Fatigue washed through her. She was exhausted, both physically and emotionally, but there was no sign yet of the helicopter, which meant they simply had to keep going.

Help us get out of here, God…

But where were they supposed to go? The cold seemed to slice all the way through her as they ran. She was pretty sure there were at least four men after them, including Jinx, and they were probably all armed. Snow crunched under her feet as they ran. Griffin might know this area well, but in the snow, with only the light of dawn, how long could they realistically keep running and evading the men behind them?

Eventually they'd be found.

"Griffin?"

"I'm okay."

"You're not okay." Tory glanced behind them and

searched the trees for signs of movement. "How far do you think they are? Because you need to stop running."

"I can't. There's a ridge about another fifty yards ahead of us where we should be able to hide. It'll give us shelter from the wind, plus a place to watch for the sheriff."

At the top of the ridge, Griffin signaled for her to stop. He walked back in their footprints, then turned in another direction and ran in a couple of circles before coming back around into the narrow space where the underbrush covered the prints, clearly hoping to throw off the men.

He grabbed her hand again. "Let's go."

He led her down the side of the rocky ledge and then pulled her with him beneath the overhang.

"If they're following our tracks, I'm hoping this way they won't be able to tell one set is a dead end, to buy us some time," he said. "We'll hunker down here under the ledge. It will give us a clear view of where the helo lands and we should be able to hear if anyone is coming from behind. It also should protect us some from the wind."

He sat next to her then tugged her against him. She could feel the heat from his body as she leaned into his chest. Could feel his warm breath against her neck. They sat still beneath the overhang, waiting as the first rays of sunlight spilled over the horizon.

"You're shaking," he said, rubbing her gloved fingers between his hands.

"I know, but you…you're the one I'm worried about."

"I'm fine. Really. Nothing more than a few bruises. I'll be back to normal in a day or two."

"Not if you damaged your rib cage further."

"What's done is done. We didn't have a choice."

"I know."

She could feel her heart pounding in her chest as they huddled silently in the semidarkness. Griffin pulled out his weapon and set it next to him. He'd told her that they didn't have enough bullets to survive a shoot-out with Jinx and his men, but clearly he wanted to be prepared. She couldn't worry about what was going to happen. For the moment she was simply grateful they were alive.

A patch of snow dropped from a branch above her and slid down her cheek. But she could barely feel it. Her face, hands and feet were numb. They needed rescuing, not just because of the men after them, but because of the dangers of exposure. She glanced at Griffin. Exposure to the elements could be just as dangerous as a bullet.

It was strange the things she could remember. Like the serious hazards of extremely low temperatures on the body, and how the stress from cold could cause things like dehydration, frostbite, numbness and hypothermia. She glanced down at her hand that felt so cold even with the gloves she was wearing. He'd been right. She was shivering, which was the first symptom of trouble for the body. Once her core temperature dropped below 98.6 degrees, the blood would begin to flow away from her arms and legs, bringing with it the risk of hypothermia.

She pushed away the medical jargon running through her mind, wishing for the moment that she'd forgotten it along with all that had happened the day she'd been out hiking.

"All of this somehow seems surreal," she said, whispering through the hazy glow of dawn. "We're watching the sun rise over a field of snow, while outlines of the mountains begin to appear. It's as if I can almost forget what's going on around me."

"I was just thinking the same thing."

But they couldn't forget. Couldn't put their guard down even for a moment. Jinx was out there, trying to follow their tracks through the snow. Finding them was inevitable. They just had to pray that the sheriff found them first.

Her breath caught at the sound of helicopter blades whirling in the distance.

"Griffin… They're here."

A rush of relief flooded through her, followed by a wave of panic. If they could hear the helicopter, so could Jinx. Once they stepped out into the open, they'd become targets for Jinx and his men. Because this wasn't over, not yet. Jinx wouldn't want them to get on that helicopter and he'd do everything in his power to stop them.

ELEVEN

Tory spotted one of the helicopter's lights as she and Griffin emerged from beneath the ledge. Jinx and his men were still somewhere behind them, but at least now they had a fighting chance of getting out alive. Griffin pulled out his flashlight and started signaling SOS at the chopper to pinpoint their location for the rescuers.

Adrenaline pressed like a weight against her chest as she watched the bird move in for a landing. She glanced behind them. They needed to get to that chopper before Jinx's men caught up to them.

A light in the chopper flashed a signal back at them.

She glanced at the ledge again. There was still no sign of Jinx or his men, but if they'd heard the chopper—which she knew they had—it wouldn't be long until they figured out exactly what was going on.

Someone yelled at them from the open door of the chopper as it landed in the clearing, but between the distance and the roar of its blades, she couldn't understand them. Shots fired behind them, above the ledge. Jinx and his men were here.

Seconds later, half a dozen men wearing bulletproof

vests exited the helicopter. Griffin squeezed her hand as two of the men crossed the clearing and headed for their location, their weapons firing into the tree line at Jinx's men as she and Griffin ran toward the helicopter.

Sheriff Jackson stopped in front of them. "We're going to get you out of here, but I need to know exactly what we're up against. How many are out there?"

"Four, maybe five." Griffin shouted above the noise from the chopper.

"Is Jinx one of them?"

"I'm pretty sure, though I never saw him." Griffin locked gazes with his brother Caden, who was one of the armed men. "What are you doing here?"

"Between my military experience and knowledge of this terrain, the sheriff asked me to help. We need to get you onto that chopper, then we're going after the men."

Griffin disagreed. "I'm glad you're here, but get her to safety and I'll come with you—"

"No way," Tory shouted. "He needs to be checked by a doctor, not out there fighting."

"What happened?" Caden asked.

"I'm fine—"

"Bruising at a minimum, but possible broken ribs as well as potential internal damage—" Tory started.

"I need to help Caden—"

"Forget it." Sheriff Jackson shot down any further arguments. "You saved her life. You've done enough. I want both of you out of here now."

Caden squeezed his brother's shoulder. "Can the two of you make it to the chopper?"

Griffin nodded. "We're good to go."

"On my signal," the sheriff said, "stay down and move as fast as you can in front of me."

She understood the unspoken implications. The worst-case scenario running through her mind was for this to somehow turn into a hostage situation or a shoot-out. Neither of which they could let happen. On top of that, in the clearing they were going to be exposed by the lack of tree cover.

The sheriff said something into his radio then turned to them. "Let's go…now."

Tory's heart pounded as she ran with Griffin in front of Caden and the sheriff toward the clearing and the chopper. The officers continued firing a steady round of bullets around them, keeping Jinx and his men pinned behind the tree line. All she could do at this point was trust that they knew what they were doing. Because while the lawmen had managed to keep Jinx and his men back in the woods, she wasn't sure how long that was going to last. Both sides were motivated, and in the balance hung her life along with Griffin's and the officers'.

They were in the middle of the clearing where the bird had touched down when she stumbled on a thick branch covered with snow. Tory very quickly regained her balance as she tried to keep her vision focused on the men waiting for them ahead and not on the men wanting her dead behind them.

She felt Griffin's arm tighten around her waist as they kept running. Another twenty yards…fifteen. She knew he had to be in pain and hoped she was wrong about the possibility of a cracked rib, but there was nothing she could do for him right now. Another ten yards and they'd be there.

Seconds later someone pulled her into the chopper and then reached for Griffin. He groaned as he climbed into the bird, but they'd made it. She glanced out the cargo door again, expecting to see Jinx and his men emerge, but there was still no sign of them. They had to be there, regrouping near the tree line. Apparently even Jinx was smart enough not to go against the firepower that had to be on this chopper.

"Get them out of here," the sheriff shouted at the pilot and his copilot in the cockpit. "We're going to take these guys down."

She caught Griffin's frown as Caden gave them a thumbs-up, but she was glad he wasn't bucking orders. Not only did he not have a vest on, his body wasn't ready physically for a confrontation like the one the men were about to face.

"Go…go…go…"

The deputies and agents were shouting at Jinx and his men. Demanding they put down their weapons. The helicopter rose from the ground, heading away from the fight as the sheriff and his men took off after Jinx. She latched her seat belt then slid on the headset, knowing how bad Griffin wanted to be on the ground taking down Jinx and his men and putting an end to all of this.

She took his wrist and checked his pulse to monitor his breathing. A punctured lung could lead to lower oxygen levels and heart function, translating to increased heart rate. For the moment, his seemed normal.

"Welcome aboard. I'm Captain Peterson, and this is Tactical Flight Officer Harper." The pilot spoke through the headsets as he took off from their landing spot. "Sit back and relax… We're going to get both of you out of here in one piece."

Sit back and relax.

Really?

She wasn't going to be able to relax until Jinx was back behind bars and all of this mess was over.

She turned to Griffin, worried about how he was doing on top of everything. "How's the pain?"

"Feels like I've been beat up, but honestly it's about the same."

"Shortness of breath or light-headedness?"

"Breathing in hurts, but it's not unbearable."

She heard a loud pop and felt a sharp pinch on her arm. She looked down and pulled up her sleeve. There was a thin stream of blood running down her forearm.

"Are you okay?" Griffin asked.

"I don't know…" The chopper took a dive to the right as she spoke. "Something just hit me."

Griffin shouted at the cockpit, but their pilot now sat slumped over in his chair. "What's going on?"

"A bullet just struck the helo and the engine failed." Officer Harper's voice was laced with panic. "And Captain Peterson… I think that bullet hit him."

Griffin yanked off his seat belt. "Can you land this bird without crashing?"

"I'm lowering the pitch now. I'll have to do a no-power landing, which is possible but tricky. What about Peterson?"

Tory was right behind him. "I'm an ER nurse. I'll do everything I can."

Griffin worked quickly with Tory to unstrap the pilot's safety belts and lie him on the floor behind the pilot seats so she could determine his status.

His face had turned ashen and both his breathing and pulse were rapid.

"He's losing too much blood," she said. "See if you can find me a first-aid kit with some clean gauze or bandages."

The chopper was rolling back and forth as the tactical officer fought to keep them level, but Griffin couldn't worry about a crash-landing. Not yet. Instead he braced himself, pulled the first-aid kit off the cabin ceiling and set it down beside her.

"I need you to try to keep him as immobile as you can, so I can work on him."

Griffin fought to keep the man as still as possible as she tore open the pilot's shirt to gain access to his chest where the blood was spreading from the slug that had embedded in his side.

"How bad is it?" he asked.

"Bad. I have to stop the bleeding…"

The bird dropped the final few feet then smashed against the ground. Griffin's back slammed against the back of the pilot's seat as silence enclosed them. He glanced around. Somehow the helo was still intact. But this wasn't over yet.

He reached out and touched her arm. "Tory…"

She nodded up at him. "I'm okay."

"Harper?"

"So am I."

"I'm impressed with your flying skills," Tory said, "but we've still got a serious problem. I'm working to get the bleeding stopped, but we need a way out of here. If he doesn't get into surgery soon, we're going to lose him."

"Do whatever it takes to save him. Please." Harper fumbled at the dials in the front seat. "Radio seems to be working. I need to go out there and make sure there's no chance this bird can catch fire. Can you let Dispatch know where we are?"

Harper gave him their coordinates then headed out into the cold. A moment later Griffin was talking to a dispatcher in Timber Falls.

"What's your status?"

"The helo was hit on our way out. The pilot was shot and we crash-landed," Griffin said.

"How's that even possible?"

"I'm not sure. I heard a loud pop…there were shards of metal debris." He looked down at the back of his hand where a piece of metal must have hit. He hadn't even noticed it before. "Somehow the bullet hit a critical point then hit the pilot."

"Do you have your location?"

Griffin passed on the coordinates.

"An ambulance should be able to make it to you on one of the gravel roads on the edge of the property now that the weather has calmed down."

"Go ahead and alert the hospital that we're coming. What about an ETA?"

"I'd estimate at least thirty minutes."

That meant an hour before they got the man to the hospital. At least they were near the road, but he could tell by the look in Tory's eyes that she wasn't sure the pilot would make it.

"Keep this channel open," the dispatcher said. "Call if there are any changes."

"Copy that."

Griffin moved to the other side of the chopper, which was perched at an angle, ignoring his own pain. "What can I do?"

"He's stabilized. For now. I need to maintain pressure on the wound for another few minutes to ensure the blood clots, but we have to get him to a hospital. The good thing is that the bullet didn't hit an artery, but there is no way for me to know what kind of internal damage we're looking at."

"One thing at a time, Tory."

"You're the next person on my list and I'd like to check out the copilot, as well."

"I'm fine," Griffin said. "Really."

"Are you always so stubborn, Deputy O'Callaghan?"

"Probably."

"Get me some snow in the meantime. It's the next best thing to an ice pack and will help close the damaged blood vessels. See if you can find some plastic to wrap it in."

"You got it."

Griffin found a plastic bag then carefully jumped out of the helo to get some snow. A minute later—task completed—he climbed back inside. A sharp pain shot through his rib cage.

"Wow…slow down." Tory moved to his side. "What are you feeling?"

"Something just…caught. But it's nothing. I'm just a bit sore."

"It's not nothing, but give me a minute."

He watched as she quickly worked on the captain, impressed with her focus on what she was doing. Because of career choices, they'd both regularly experienced how fragile life was, and knew the pain that went with facing losing someone they were trying to save. It was something that had shaped him as a person and no doubt had done the same to her.

She shifted toward him. "Let me look at you now. I've told you before that there's a good chance you've got a broken rib."

He shoved aside another stubborn reply and complied.

Tory pressed her fingers against his rib cage. "Does that hurt?"

"Yes."

He drew away, but not because of the pain. Her hands felt cold against his side, but it wasn't cold he was forcing himself to ignore. It was her nearness. He'd always been so good at guarding his heart. Why couldn't he do it with her around?

Her hands pressed again a couple of inches lower. This time he just grimaced at the pain.

"Ow."

"Does that hurt?"

"A little, but mainly because your hands are freezing."

"Funny."

"Do you think anything's broken?"

"We need to get you either an X-ray or CT scan to know for sure. A bit of snow might help ease the pain for you, as well, while we wait."

The distant sounds of a siren whirred in the background as Harper slipped back into the cockpit. "Ambulance is almost here. How is the captain?"

"I've done everything I can and he's stable for the moment, but he needs to get to a hospital."

Five minutes later Griffin was watching the paramedics move the captain into the back of the ambulance, while Tory insisted he stay out of the way so he wouldn't put any pressure on his ribs. He knew she was probably right, but he hated how out of control he felt. This was supposed to have been a simple task of guarding a witness. Instead they'd barely made it out alive, the pilot was fighting for his life and now Caden, along with the sheriff, were on the ground trying to take down Jinx.

That wasn't all that he was worried about. He watched Tory follow the paramedics, explaining what she'd done, and tried to curb the emotions running through him. He hadn't expected his heart to get tangled up in all of this, but there was no way to ignore the worry pulsing through him. He shifted his gaze to the crashed helo. They needed to put an end to this now, before someone else got hurt.

TWELVE

Tory walked down the wide hallway of the regional hospital, thankful for the jeans, boots and sweater someone had scrounged up for her to replace what she'd been wearing. An ER doctor had looked at her leg and assured her that it seemed her amnesia would clear up without treatment. He let her go with a security detail only three steps behind her. Now she needed to find out what was going on with Griffin. He'd walked into this nightmare and risked his own life to save hers.

"Tory!"

She turned around to see Caden hurrying to catch up with her. "You're back."

Caden stopped in front of her. "Thankfully, we all made it without any serious injuries."

"We heard you made two arrests, but not Jinx."

"Unfortunately, Jinx and Max got away on one of the snowmobiles. The FBI are questioning the men they arrested right now, but I'm not sure we'll get anything out of them. These guys are loyal lapdogs."

"The weather might have slowed everything down, but they'll find him. He can't go far."

At least, that's what she wanted to believe. While it might be true, there were dozens of places he could hunker down and stay hidden, and Jinx had already spent plenty of time evading the authorities to know exactly how to do it.

She rubbed her hands together, still feeling the chill that seemed to have gone all the way through her and refused to leave. "Do you have any news on the pilot or Griffin? I was on my way to find Griffin."

"He's going to be fine. The good news is that there aren't any broken ribs, and no signs of internal damage, though he's going to be pretty sore the next few days."

"I'm relieved."

"Me, too. In fact, you can see him. They've decided he won't have to be admitted."

"That's good news," she said. "What about the pilot?"

"He's still in surgery. Unfortunately that's all I know."

"What happens now?"

"I spoke briefly to the lead FBI agent. They want you to go into protective custody until they find Jinx."

She glanced back at her FBI security detail. "And if they don't find him? I can't just hide forever."

"You'll have to talk to them, but they'll find him. He has nowhere else to run. He's trapped out there in that wilderness with the entire state looking for him. They'll get him. I promise."

She wanted to believe him, but she'd heard that before. And while she didn't want anyone else getting hurt, she needed to return to her own life, as well.

"I know that both the sheriff and the FBI will want to talk to you," Caden said, "but why don't you go see Griffin first. They're arranging transport to a safe house, and I've sent someone to get your stuff from the ranch."

"Thank you. I appreciate it. Everything."

"Not a problem."

She started to walk toward the ER then stopped and turned back to Caden. "Can I ask you something?"

"Of course."

"Is Griffin well enough to be on my guard detail?"

The words came out of her mouth before she'd taken the time to think them through. She had no right to ask something like that, but despite everything that had happened, she felt safe when he was with her. And feeling safe was what she needed right now.

"I'm sorry." She waved her hand at him. "Forget it. I shouldn't have asked that. He's been through enough and this case…it doesn't involve him. I guess I was just hoping for someone…familiar. But he never should have had to guard me in the first place. I'm pretty sure he wishes at this point he'd never agreed to the assignment."

Caden let out a low laugh. "Then you don't know Griffin that well yet. He's the kind of man who would go the extra mile for a stranger and never look back. So believe me when I say he doesn't regret anything that happened other than the fact that you had to go through what you did. Trust me on that one."

"Still—"

"I think it's a good idea, and as long as the doctor agrees that he's still medically fit, I can ask the FBI for you if you'd like, though I have no idea if they'd approve something like that."

"I understand. Thank you."

"And, Tory… I'm glad you're okay. Both of you."

"Thanks. Me, too."

She hurried down the hallway, wanting to take back her rash words. She never should have asked that of Caden. Griffin hadn't really had a choice the first time, but he did now. Asking him to put his life at risk wasn't fair. This wasn't his case. She wasn't his problem.

Something she was going to have to remember.

Griffin was sitting up on a bed behind one of the curtains, his left cheek and eye a colorful mixture of blue and purple. He smiled when he saw her, shooting a pulse of adrenaline through her.

"I heard you have good news," she said. "No broken bones."

"Doctor says I'll live…just some bumps and bruises. What about you?"

"I've finally warmed up…" She rubbed her hands together. "For the most part, anyway."

"And emotionally?"

She hesitated at his question. "I won't try to pretend that this hasn't shaken me up. My memory is still lagging behind and I can't recall anything about that day."

"Does the doctor have any concerns?"

"He believes I'll be fine in a few days. At least physically."

"That's good." He reached out and squeezed her hand. "I'm just so sorry about all of this. My job was to protect you—"

"You're sorry." She felt his hand enclose hers. "You saved my life, Griffin. None of this was your fault. I don't think anyone realized how relentless that man is."

"As long as you're okay, that's all that matters at this

point." He pulled up the edge of his sheet. "Though I have to say, you're full of a few surprises, as well. Rappelling down from the catwalk on the watchtower was no easy feat."

She matched his smile. "You were pretty impressive yourself."

"Thanks, though I can't help but wonder how damaged the fire tower is. It seems insignificant in the light of everything that's happened, but it still makes me sad."

"It was a part of your heritage and a piece of your childhood. Something your grandfather left behind."

"Do you know what they're planning to do next?"

"I haven't spoke to the FBI yet, but your brother told me that they want to put me into protective custody until they arrest him."

Griffin grabbed his jacket off the chair beside the bed. "I need to talk with the sheriff. I want to be out there looking for him."

"You need to rest."

"The doctor says I'm fine. I'm just waiting for them to fill a prescription, but no broken ribs, and thankfully no signs of infection in my arm. As soon as the doctor signs my release, I'm out of here. I want to help find this man."

"You're both right." The sheriff walked into the room. "You need to rest, but I also need your help."

Griffin moved his legs over to the edge of the bed. "Anything."

"Caden will be here in a few minutes. I've asked for his help, as well." Sheriff Jackson laid a paper map on the bed and let out a low laugh. "We're going low-tech, but the bottom line is that we need your expertise to find Jinx. If Max is with him, there's a good chance they're hiding out on the property until this weather clears. We have to figure out where he might be. You and Caden know the ranch better than anyone. We're coordinating with the FBI and have roadblocks set up along all the major roads leading out from the ranch and the surrounding property. But in your opinion, what's his most likely hideout?"

Tory took a step back as Griffin and the sheriff started going over the map, feeling the tendrils of fear around her heart lessen slightly. Jinx might still be out there, but they weren't done fighting.

Griffin stared at the map as his mind formulated an answer for the sheriff. "With a canyon on the southwest side, and highlands surrounding most of the rest of the ranch, access is limited. There are really only two easy exit points."

He pointed to two spots on the map before continuing.

"On top of that, there aren't a lot of places where they could wait out the weather besides the main house and staff houses. There's an equipment barn, a workshop and our cattle handling facilities to the west. Beyond them, there are a couple hunting cabins they could hole up in as well as several hunting blinds. There's also the feed and supply shelter where they took us, and of course the fire tower. But I don't think there's much of that left."

The sheriff took a step back. "So, if you were Jinx, having to deal with both this weather and the knowledge of being a wanted man, what would you do? Especially considering you have someone with you who knows the land like the back of his hand. Even if they decide to wait out the end of the storm, they will have to emerge eventually."

Griffin glanced at Caden, who'd just stepped into the room. "I don't know what my brother would say, but I'd get as far away from here as possible."

"I agree." Caden stopped at the end of the bed. "He's got a snowmobile, which means his best bet is slipping off the property and heading out of state. If I were him, I'd avoid Denver and opt for somewhere like Albuquerque or Wichita where he could then potentially leave the country."

Griffin nodded at his brother's input. "There will be issues trying to maneuver cross-country with a snowmobile. Not only are there only a couple of routes out, there are also fallen trees because of the storm. We saw that firsthand."

The sheriff stared at the map. "Then what are their obvious routes?"

"Besides the main road, which I think we'd all agree they'll avoid, they could go over the highlands toward Mountain Springs," Caden said. "There's also a route through the canyon toward Canyon Falls, but that would be foolish this time of year."

Griffin glanced at his brother, convinced that was exactly what Jinx and his men were going to avoid. "With Max guiding him, they'll stay away from the obvious routes."

"Agreed," Caden said. "That means the only other real option is to have someone fly in and get them. Jinx has resources. We know that by now. He could arrange for an extraction, like we did with a helicopter. There's an unpaved runway just south of the fire tower. It hasn't been used for years, but the last time I checked it out, it was usable."

"Good. I'll make sure we're watching the airways," Sheriff Jackson confirmed. "Are there any other routes they might take?"

"There is one other option." Griffin studied the map, trying to formulate what he'd do if he were Jinx. "We know two things about Jinx. One, he's a risk taker. Not only did he manage to escape from his prison transport, he also has lots of outside connections. He wouldn't have gone in there to find us if he didn't have a way out."

"That makes sense."

"That means we have to assume he's willing to take a risk if he believes it will get him out of there without getting caught."

Sheriff Jackson folded his arms across his chest. "So what would you do?"

"If I were them, I'd head north across the land here." He pointed to a spot on the map. "Like I said, it's risky—it goes through some pretty rough terrain— but the trail is wide enough for a snowmobile."

"I think you're right." Caden moved to the other side of the bed to get closer to the map. "We used to take that route when we were teens. It avoids all the main roads and ends up at Beeker's Crossing, which is on the border of the next ranch."

"Exactly." Griffin nodded then turned to the sheriff. "Have you got anyone patrolling this section?"

The sheriff shook his head.

"There's an off-road trail that connects the two properties and eventually leads to Highway 24," Griffin noted.

"Where we wouldn't even be looking for them." Sheriff Jackson's frown deepened. "I didn't think that road was very accessible this time of year."

"All they'd need is someone to pick them up in a 4x4, then they could easily disappear into the next ranch, head south and—"

The sheriff concluded, "We'd lose him."

"Exactly. If he doesn't decide to hunker down another day or so, which in my mind is unlikely at this point, he's going to want to get as far away as possible. This route would work and Max would know about it."

Griffin glanced at Tory before looking back at the sheriff and adding, "There is one other thing."

"What's that?"

"I meant what I said. I want to help. I might be a bit sore, but that won't stop me, and the doctor has cleared me. I'm just waiting for a prescription."

Sheriff Jackson frowned. "The doctor might have cleared you, but I haven't. Not for fieldwork."

"I've got a few bruises," Griffin said, "nothing more."

"I do have something in mind I thought you could handle, though."

"What's that?"

"It was your brother's idea."

"I'm interested."

"I can put you on Tory's protection detail. The FBI's still stretched thin because of this storm. If you're interested, that is."

He looked at Tory and smiled. "Like I said. I'm interested."

"Good—"

"Wait a minute." Tory took a step forward. "Griffin, you have nothing to prove to me or anyone else. I'd rather you take care of yourself. You need to rest—"

"Forget it. There's no way I can sit around waiting for the aches and pains to disappear. I need to be out there doing something." He caught her gaze and winked. "Even if it means babysitting this feisty nurse I just met."

She rolled her eyes at him but there was something else in her expression that he couldn't read.

"Then it's settled." Sheriff Jackson folded up his map, interrupting Griffin's thoughts. "A car will be here to pick the two of you up and take you to a safe house in the next hour. Thankfully the roads are being cleared, so you should be able to get there with no problems. In the meantime, I'll coordinate with the team and make sure we're ready."

Griffin waited until both the sheriff and his brother had left the room before turning back to Tory.

"Are you okay? I know these past couple of days have been difficult, not just physically, but emotionally, as well. And while you might be trained to deal with trauma, facing it personally is entirely different. There's a lot you'll have to process."

"I know, and I plan to deal with it, but that's not what I'm worried about right now."

His brow furrowed. "What do you mean?"

She stared out the window a few seconds before turning back around. "Having you join my protection team wasn't Caden's idea. It was mine."

"Really?"

He was surprised and couldn't help but wonder what the implications meant, but he wasn't going to go there. Not yet.

"I'm glad you asked."

"Because you like babysitting?"

He shot her a smile. "Not particularly, but I like you."

She shrugged, as if dismissing his comment. A comment that had come out far too…personal.

"You've done more than your part in all of this," she said. "And now look what happened out there. You could be dead. We could both be dead."

"But we're not." He reached out and grasped her hands. "You have nothing to feel guilty about. I didn't go into this blindly, and just because things got tough doesn't mean I'm planning to walk away. And somehow, I don't think I have much to worry about, hanging out with you in an FBI safe house."

"Jinx has done tougher things than track me down in a safe house—"

"And if he tries, he's going to regret the day he decided to mess with me." He squeezed her hand before letting it go, wishing he didn't notice the slight tilt of her mouth or the subtle scent of vanilla in her hair that still mingled with the smell of the fire.

"I don't think I've ever met anyone quite like you, Griffin O'Callaghan."

"And I could definitely say the same about you. Besides…" He let out a low laugh. "I'm waiting for your memory to come back so I can get to know you better."

"Griffin… Tory…"

Griffin's attention shifted to the other side of the room. "Mom… Dad…"

"The sheriff's been keeping us updated. We've been so worried about you. Decided to come to work because there was nothing I could do."

He pulled his parents into a big hug, knowing that the worry never went away, especially with four grown boys who had a habit of putting themselves in the line of fire.

His mom looked up and caught his gaze. "What happened?"

"They were able to extract us from the scene, but somehow a bullet hit the helo and the pilot. We shouldn't be alive, but the tactical officer managed to land the bird safely."

"And you're sure you're okay," his father said.

"I look far worse for wear. The doctor says I'll be fine."

"What about you?" His mother turned to Tory. "I've been frantic the past few hours worrying about both of you."

"I'm fine." Tory gave her a hesitant smile. "Still shook up over the experience, but I'll be okay."

"And your memory?" Griffin's father asked.

"It's slowly coming back, though I still have no memory of what happened the day I witnessed the murder. It's blank."

"Your cheeks are red and you look so cold. We need to get you warmed up." Marci pressed the back of her hand against Tory's face. "And the men who took you both… They've proved they aren't above stopping anyone who stands in their way."

"That's why we're making sure there is a protection detail around her at all times," Griffin said.

Sheriff Jackson walked back into the curtained room, interrupting their conversation. "I've got some bad news."

Griffin frowned. "Like things could actually get worse than they already are?"

"We think your guess as to where Jinx and Max were headed was spot on."

Griffin hesitated before asking the next logical question. "Why?"

"Because we just found Max's body in a gully about three miles south of Beeker's Crossing."

Griffin nodded. "And Jinx?"

Sheriff Jackson's jaw tightened. "Jinx has vanished again."

THIRTEEN

Griffin set a plate of hamburger and fries on the coffee table in front of Tory before sitting across from her with his lunch. "There's also potato salad and lemonade."

"Thank you." She popped one of the fries into her mouth, grateful he'd agreed to be a part of her security detail. "I didn't know I was so hungry, but you could probably hear my stomach rumbling from across the room."

"I'm just glad you're eating."

"That's not a problem. I'm pretty sure I tend to eat when I'm stressed." She took a bite of the burger. "And this just might be the best burger I've ever had."

"Good."

She took another bite and felt a dollop of mayo fall on her chin. "Don't even laugh."

"Trust me, I don't want to. Laughing—and movement, for that matter—hurts too much."

He smiled at her as she grabbed a napkin, reminding Tory how much she liked the way his smile reached his eyes.

She grabbed another fry. "Thanks for being here."

"I'm just relieved to know that we're here and not out there in that freezing weather."

She glanced around the hotel room the FBI had escorted them to on the outskirts of Denver. While she might not be home, at least she felt safe. It was a typical cookie-cutter living room with a connecting bedroom, both with brown walls and dated pictures on the wall. But none of that mattered. All she really cared about was that it was far from Jinx and his men and the danger they'd been exposed to over the last couple days. And that Griffin hadn't flinched at her request to stay on as a part of her security detail.

She took a long sip of her lemonade. "There's only one thing that's stopping us from properly celebrating."

"Jinx."

She nodded.

He was still out there. Somewhere. It was why they were sitting in the guarded hotel suite with two agents outside their door. Yet another reminder that this was far from over. A BOLO had been sent out to all law enforcement, but so far there had been no news of his arrest.

"They'll find him." Griffin said.

"Then I still have to testify," she said, unable to separate herself from the fear. "He's smart, though. What if he still gets away with everything he's done, like he has so far? With all the hurt he's caused people, if he's set loose…" A shiver slid down her spine. "Men like him don't just walk away from their lifestyle. It has to stop."

"The FBI told me they're working on a deal with the men they arrested earlier today near the watchtower. If they can get enough evidence of what Jinx has done, then maybe you won't have to testify."

"Part of that evidence will have to come from his men, but they're loyal." Tory still wasn't convinced it would be over anytime soon. "Do you really think they'll be able to turn them?"

"I can't answer that."

"And I need to protect the other witness who was with me that day."

"You still don't remember who it was?"

She shook her head. "The majority of my memories seem to be coming back, but that day—the day I saw the murders—I can't remember. There's nothing more than a few hazy flashes."

"Give yourself time." Griffin reached out and squeezed her hand. "Trauma's powerful and you've been through a lot. The rest of the memories will surface and you'll have time to deal with them. Until then, just enjoy your hamburger and the company."

Like the calm before the next storm.

She was enjoying the company, but she needed to change the subject.

"You told me a few things about Christmas in Timber Falls. What's your favorite Christmas memory?" she asked.

Her own Christmas memories were nothing more than a blurry fog; she needed something normal to focus on. Something completely opposite from everything they'd just experienced.

"Favorite Christmas memory… I definitely have one or two of those, but the best one was probably nine or ten."

She stuck a fry in her mouth and leaned back, grateful for the distraction.

"I got up early that morning, because I was convinced my parents had bought us a Nintendo. I'd been reminding them for months what I was expecting that year, so I knew there was no way they didn't know what I wanted. And, of course, I had hinted along the way every reason why they should buy it for me."

She shot him an amused smile. "So did you get it?"

"I was up extra early that year. I ran downstairs and, while the lights were twinkling, there were no presents under the tree."

"Nothing?"

"Nothing," he confirmed. "Only our stockings hanging on the fireplace mantel. I figured there had to be something pretty spectacular in them, so I looked inside."

Tory grinned. "Of course you did. And?"

His smile faded as he leaned forward to pick up his drink. "There was a lump of coal inside the toe."

"A lump of coal?" Now she couldn't help but laugh out loud. "Seriously?"

"I quickly felt the toes of all the other stockings and didn't have to look inside to realize what was there. No presents, just four stockings with coal."

"I would have loved to have seen the look on your face when you saw them."

"It was a sad Christmas morning, let me tell you, because, according to my mother—as I soon found out—all four of us had made it to the top of the naughty list that year with our constant bickering, complaining and fighting, and she'd had enough."

"Wait a minute…a lump of coal and no presents… that is your favorite Christmas memory?"

Griffin let out a deep sigh. "Definitely one of the most memorable ones, though that's not quite the end of the story."

"So what happened?"

She took a sip of her drink, loving how he not only could distract her but make her laugh. That was exactly what she needed right now. A way to forget that they were sitting in the middle of an FBI safe room with an ongoing manhunt for someone wanting to silence her.

"We ended up moping all morning until the four of us boys finally got together and decided we had about twelve hours to make things right before Christmas was over."

"You had to find a way to get back on the nice list."

"Exactly."

She sat back, plate of fries in hand, and tucked her legs beneath her. "This is going to be interesting."

"Without my mom saying another word, we started cleaning our rooms. Every inch. We vacuumed, dusted and worked to remove some old stain on the carpet. Then we moved to the bathroom, where I was reminded—not for the first time—how to use a toilet brush. Finally our parents sat us down and told us that there might be presents, if all four had learned our lesson."

"And had you?"

"I know I had. Eventually my mom decided we'd earned our keep and brought out the telescope they'd bought for us. I was mesmerized from the very beginning."

"That explains your interest in stargazing."

Griffin nodded. "We spent all night glued to the sky, not caring that the temperature was hovering near freezing or that our fingers were half frozen. And on top of that, we'd learned our lesson. All four of us."

"I had no idea that the town deputy had such a sordid past."

"I've tried to redeem myself." He smiled at her comment. "And over the months that followed, I took to searching for planets, comets and asteroids. I even thought I might study aerospace engineering one day."

"Like the view from the tower last night, there's something almost sacred about a starlit night." Tory closed her eyes for a moment. "Another of God's amazing creations that reminds me how small I am in comparison and yet with it comes the reality of both His vast power and His love for me."

"'The heavens declare the glory of God.'"

She nodded, reminded suddenly of how God hadn't left her to go through this alone.

"What about you?" he asked. "What do you want for Christmas this year? Besides getting your memories back and your life returning to normal, which in itself is a tall order. Just something for you."

She picked at a fry and contemplated her answer. "I can promise you my answer won't be nearly as amusing as your story, but as crazy as it sounds, I'd love to spend my day vacuuming and doing laundry—all those boring things everyone tries to avoid. It seems so normal and so far away right now. Though I'll leave the toilet bowl cleaning to you."

"Ha!" He took the last bite of his hamburger. "This will be over. I promise."

"I know."

"And when it is, I have an idea."

"What's that?"

He leaned forward and set down his plate. "I could be your tour guide around here for a couple days. A few walks in the mountains, a trip on the Royal Gorge Route Railroad and, if the stars are clear, I've still got that old telescope. It's all simple, but far better than doing laundry to make you forget everything."

"I think I'd like that."

She felt her cheeks warm, imaging what it would be like to spend a day doing something fun with Griffin. Imagining becoming a part of his life. But once again the gaps in her memories and the fear of what she didn't know tried to pull her back to a place of security—a place where she wasn't sure she wanted to go anymore.

Griffin pulled his gaze away from the soft blush that had just registered on Tory's face, one he was pretty sure didn't come from the warm air circulating through the vent above them. What had he been thinking? Talking to her about spending time together when all of this was over. He might as well have asked her out on a date. The problem was, it didn't matter that he felt attracted to her. He was a deputy working an FBI case and she was in his protective custody. He had a job to do and she was becoming a distraction.

"You mentioned taking a train," she said, pulling him away from his thoughts.

"Yes…?"

The stress of the past few days seemed to vanish

from Tory's eyes as she welcomed the memory. "I remember something about a favorite Christmas."

His brow rose slightly. "I'm assuming you weren't on the naughty list like I was."

"Of course not." She shot him a smile. "Anyway, I must have been... I don't know, seven, maybe eight. I was with my parents and sister and we were celebrating my mother's birthday on a train. It was Christmastime—her birthday was December twenty-fourth—and I remember we were in this restored dining car, eating on white tablecloths while all dressed up." She closed her eyes for a moment. "There were lights out the windows, Christmas music played in the background, and we must have driven through a replica of the North Pole, because I remember snow and Santa's village with all kinds of lights and a huge Christmas tree."

"Sounds beautiful."

"It was. I don't remember what we ate, though I do recall my sister and I being told we could have as much hot chocolate and cookies as we wanted after dinner." She held up the snowflake pendant he'd noticed her wearing. "My father gave my sister and me matching necklaces for Christmas that year."

He settled back into his corner of the couch, enjoying the chance to learn something new about her. His mom had told Caden she thought Tory was beautiful and charming. Both were true. And his brother had been right about another thing. Griffin had felt lost. For a long time. And it wasn't just because he felt like there was something missing in his life...like a wife and a family. He'd been quick this whole time to dismiss the possibility of pursuing something with Tory, but why shouldn't he? There were not rules against a sheriff's deputy falling for a witness. Reality bore through him like a knife, because there was still something he could never forget, and that was Lilly and how he'd failed her.

"What are you thinking?" she asked.

He looked at her, knowing there was no way he could tell her the truth. "Just that you seem to finally be relaxing."

"I think it's helping my memory, as well. I don't feel as if I'm running for my life."

"I want you to feel safe."

"I do." She grabbed the throw pillow between them and pulled it against her chest. "But I've also been thinking about how you and I both deal with trauma. We're always the ones facing it head-on to save someone. But now, for the first time, I'm on the other side. This…" She glanced around the room. "All of this is so personal."

"I know it's been hard."

"You probably still feel it with every breath. Thank you."

"For what?"

"For being here. For listening to me. For making me believe I'm not losing it."

He smiled. "You're not losing it."

"I know, but when you can't remember who you are, down to the little details of what you like for breakfast, or where you shop for groceries, or even your favorite Christmas memory…it's frightening. I've never felt so out of control as I do right now." She looked up and caught his gaze. "And there's nothing I can do beyond sitting back, waiting and trusting other people with my life."

"I can think of a few times when you've done a bit more than sit back and wait. You rappelled down a burning fire tower without a harness, worked to save a man's life in the middle of a helicopter crash… You're an amazing woman, Tory, and I—"

He stopped midsentence.

I don't want you to leave after this is over.

There was no way to ignore the fact that he was falling for her, which never should have happened. He never should have made this personal. Never tried to mix his work with his feelings. But he had. His gaze dropped to her lips. He wanted to lean over and kiss her, to tell her exactly what he was feeling. How the more he got to know her, the more he wanted to know the things that were still lost. But not now. For her safety, and that of his own, he couldn't let his guard down.

"I almost forgot," he said, abruptly changing the subject. "I have something for you. Caden gave me a laptop to use in case we need to catch up on emails or Facebook. We can't send messages or post anything for now, but at least it's a way to check on things. And who knows? Maybe something will spark some more memories."

She hesitated, as if digging into an evasive memory. "I don't think I have a Facebook account."

"Everyone has a Facebook account."

"I'm pretty sure I don't."

"Why do you think that?" he asked.

"I remember a conversation I had with my sister. We were arguing about how she thought it was such a great place to keep up with her friends—which I agree—but I told her I'd far rather keep up with my friends in person. She thought I was crazy."

"So no posting photos of your cat or what you had for dinner?"

"Apparently not."

"You have email, don't you?"

She shot him a dirty look. "Everyone has an email address, and believe it or not, I think I even know my password."

He handed her the laptop. "Then why don't you start? Caden will contact anyone who needs an update on you."

"I appreciate it. I'm sure my boss and my friends would want that."

He watched her read through her emails, content in the comfortable quiet that had settled between them.

A frown settled across her lips as she studied the screen.

"Is everything okay?"

"Just an overflowing amount of junk mail, like normal. I'll deal with the rest later." She closed the lid and set the laptop between them. "If you don't mind, I think I'm going to go lie down. I didn't realize how tired I was until it hit me just now."

"Of course. Are you sure you're okay?"

"Yeah."

"Why don't you sleep for a while? I'll be here if you need anything."

"I know, and I appreciate it. Everything you've done."

Her abrupt exit surprised him. Before she left, he caught her gaze and tried to read her expression, but all he could see was the fatigue. Maybe she was just tired. He picked up the laptop as soon as the door to her room shut and tried to check what she'd been looking at, but she'd erased the browser's history.

What had she seen? What was she hiding from him?

He tried to dismiss his apprehensions. She was a private person and certainly didn't owe him an explanation of everything she did.

Then why did his gut tell him something was very wrong?

FOURTEEN

Tory stepped into her room and quickly shut the door behind her. She drew in a deep breath and tried to steady her nerves. She'd only told Griffin the partial truth, leaving out the email she'd received from *him*.

I have your sister.

Somehow the unthinkable had happened.

A flood of memories exploded to the surface. The image of red hair, freckles and a bright smile resurfaced. Days horseback riding in the mountains…violin lessons…pink ballet skirts…high school graduation….

It was all coming back to her. Elizabeth had been with her that day. And if she didn't find a way to stop them, she'd lose her.

Tory replayed the message in her mind while a sliver of fear dug deeper. No police or FBI. Not even Griffin.

Or her sister would die.

She couldn't let that happen.

She'd memorized the address Jinx had given her because it was the only way to save her sister. Her life for her sister's. She'd gladly pay that price. But what guarantees were there that he'd keep her sister safe if she showed up?

She ran through her choices, thankful Griffin wasn't there with her. She'd never be able to hide the truth from him. Her resolve waivered as she glanced toward the closed door. She should tell him what was going on. He might be able to find a way to locate Jinx and save her sister, but was that a chance she could afford?

No.

Jinx was smart. She'd seen how he worked and knew the hold he had on his men. They'd do anything he said and, because of it, he'd managed to arrange a prison escape, the takedown of an FBI detail and then later had them kidnapped out of Griffin's house. So far, for whatever reason, the authorities continued to be a step behind. And for that reason, she couldn't take the risk of anything happening to Elizabeth.

She had to do what he said; her only objective right now was to protect Elizabeth. It was the reason her sister's name hadn't been mentioned in the FBI file. The reason Tory was here right now. And if there was a mole in the FBI, telling Griffin would only ensure the plan got back to Jinx. Another risk she refused to take.

She grabbed the phone book from the desk drawer and looked up the number for a taxi. She still wasn't sure how she was going to do this without Griffin figuring out her plan, or what she'd do once she got to the address Jinx had given her, but she'd deal with the problems one at a time.

Memories of the day she'd witnessed the murders suddenly engulfed her. It was as if the places she hadn't been able to breach had finally come into view. She could smell the pine trees and feel the sun as they'd hiked up the trail. Elizabeth had wanted to leave the path to get a better photo of the valley below. Then she'd seen it. The glint of sun on the barrel of the gun as the bearded man pointed it at the couple. She'd heard them plead for their lives. Heard him laugh. Heard the gunshot. That man had snatched away their lives then tossed them over the cliff like yesterday's trash.

Now that the floodgates had been opened, there was no way she could go back. She needed to get out of her room without Griffin knowing where she was going, but security was tight on this level. She glanced at the window, going through her options again. She quickly crossed the room, unlocked the window latch and pulled it up. Cold air rushed into the room, though the window would only open about four inches. She glanced at the parking lot five stories below. It didn't matter. With no balcony and no ledge, it wasn't an option.

She was going to have to walk out.

Tory sat at the small desk, called the taxi for a pickup two blocks away. She had fifty dollars in cash and a couple of credit cards in her wallet. She knew she couldn't use the cards and hoped the fifty would cover the taxi fare. She searched her memory for the layout of the hotel as she glanced around her room and then pulled on her sweater. If she wore her coat, Griffin would notice.

"I'm going to grab something sweet from the vending machine," she said, stepping out of her room.

He looked up from the book he'd been reading. "If you're hungry I could order a pizza."

She shook her head. "Thanks, but I'm craving something sweet and can just grab something from the machine."

"Couldn't sleep?"

"A bit restless, I guess."

Tory shot him a smile and tried to look relaxed, hoping he didn't notice that her palms were sweating and her heart was racing. Because she was anything but relaxed. Her heart was screaming at her to tell him exactly what was going on. That it was foolish to try to rescue her sister on her own.

"Are you sure you're okay?"

"Yeah. My sweet tooth is just kicking in. Stress, I suppose." She glanced at the clock. Every second that ticked by was another second her sister was with Jinx. "I'll probably read a little bit then fall asleep. I'm exhausted, but maybe too exhausted to sleep."

"I found a deck of cards if you're in a competitive mood?"

"Thanks." She forced another smile. "But I don't think I have the energy for that."

"Okay."

She forced herself to pause at the door leading to the hallway. "Do you want any from the vending machine?"

"No, thanks. Just make sure one of the agents goes with you."

"I'll be fine, Griffin—"

"Just do it for me."

She stepped out into the hallway where the two agents in suits were seated outside their door, arguing about chances of the Broncos winning this season's Super Bowl.

"Evening, gentleman. I'm just going to grab a candy bar from the vending machine and will be right back."

The heavyset one started to stand, but she waved him back to his seat.

"It's thirty feet away. I'm pretty sure I'll be fine."

Her heart pounded as she started walking down the hall and then slipped around the corner to where the ice machine and vending machine were located. She shoved a dollar into the machine and pushed one of the buttons, not caring what it spewed out. She'd already decided that the stairwell was going to be her best and fastest option. She listened for footsteps, but clearly they didn't seem to think anything was odd about her sweet tooth. They were still talking about football.

As the candy bar thumped into the bottom of the vending machine, Tory pushed open the stairwell door then made sure it didn't slam behind her. A second later she was running down the stairs to the lobby. She wasn't worried about hotel cameras. It would only take Griffin a minute, maybe two, to realize something was wrong. That meant she needed to put as much distance as possible between them in the short time that she had.

More memories surfaced as she made it to the fourth-floor landing. She'd sat in a small room with two FBI agents, talking to them about what she'd seen as they tried to convince her to be a witness. But there were questions she couldn't ignore.

What if they find out about Elizabeth? I'll risk my life, but I won't risk hers.

Anonymity is hard these days with social media, but there are things we can do—

I don't have a Facebook account, if that's what you're

worried about. She's my stepsister so we have different last names and live in different parts of town.

You don't have a Facebook account?

I know. I'm one of the few holdouts. I just never took the time to jump on the bandwagon.

That will make it easier to ensure there is no con-nection. And on top of that, we can keep her out of any communication and reports. There won't be any way for them to connect her to you. She'll be safe.

Tory shoved open the door and stepped into a hall-way off the main lobby. The FBI had clearly been wrong. What she didn't know was if Jinx knew the whole truth. Because after all this time, she finally re-membered the secret she'd been guarding with her life.

Her sister was the other witness.

Griffin glanced at his watch and frowned. Two min-utes was more than enough time to grab a candy bar out of a vending machine. He tried to stuff down the ensuing worry, but he couldn't help it. Maybe he was simply being paranoid, but she was his responsibility.

He waited another fifteen seconds then headed out into the hallway where the two agents sat, guarding the room.

"Where is she?"

The men looked up from their seats. "She went to get a candy bar—"

"And you didn't go with her?" Griffin started down the hallway toward the vending and ice machines.

"She said she'd be fine." One of them scrambled down the hall behind him.

Of course she did.

He ran around the corner to the small alcove and froze. A chocolate bar sat in the bottom of the vending machine, but there was no sign of her.

His heart plummeted as he shouted back at the agents. "Call it in. We need to find her. Now."

Agent Nevett started barking off a bunch of orders. "Head to the lobby, Deputy. Check with staff and camera surveillance. We'll implement a search of the hotel."

Griffin nodded and started down the stairwell toward the lobby. He'd caught the flicker of fear in her eyes as she'd walked away earlier. Why hadn't he asked her what was wrong? Whatever it was, all that mattered was finding her before Jinx did. Assuming the man didn't already have her.

He rushed past the third-floor landing. That Jinx was here, somewhere, was the obvious answer. But how would he have lured her out? There were only two real options. Either Jinx or one of his men had grabbed her or he'd found some kind of leverage that had motivated Tory to walk out of the hotel on her own.

Her sister.

It was the one thing that made sense. He'd seen the fear in her eyes. The excuse of needing something sweet...

It was the one move that would have induced her to walk out of this hotel without telling him. He replayed what had happened in the hotel room as he made it to the second floor. She'd been going through her emails. When she'd given him back the laptop, she'd erased her history. That had to be the reason. Jinx had found a way to get to her despite the strict security measures they'd put into place. But that still didn't tell him where she'd gone.

At the bottom of the stairs, he pushed open the door that led into the busy lobby. The hotel was hosting two conferences over the weekend, a technology forum and a nursing conference, which meant the restaurant, bar and lobby were full. He searched the areas carefully, but didn't see her anywhere. If Jinx was behind this, Griffin was certain the man would want to get her as far away as possible from the hotel. He'd know that they'd automatically start a thorough search of the facility, so his best option was to either transport her himself or have her meet him at a location.

But where? That was what they had to determine.

Griffin signaled to the hotel manager and pulled him away from the busy front desk before showing the man his badge. "The woman I was with is missing."

"What happened?"

"We're not sure, but I need to know if you or anyone else saw her leave," he said, then quickly gave him Tory's description.

"I'm sorry, but I've been working at the front desk. I can ask my staff who are on this floor."

"Do it. And I'll also need to see your camera footage for the past ten minutes."

"Of course. I'll get you set up right now."

While the manager spoke with his staff, Griffin sat in the office in front of a computer screen and started watching the camera footage from the past ten minutes.

Bingo.

He found her, but it only showed her walking across the lobby toward a side door. Then nothing.

"I'm sorry." The hotel manager's frown deepened. "I called together the floor staff, and I wish I could tell you more, but so far no one remembers seeing her."

Griffin sat back in the chair, trying to put the pieces of the puzzle together as Agent Nevett stepped into the room.

"Did you find her?" Griffin asked.

"No, but we've got officers searching floor by floor."

"She's not in the building. She's long gone." Griffin showed the agent the video footage of her leaving the building as his mind continued to work through her movements. Something on that laptop had triggered this, and he had to find out what it was.

He turned back to the manager. "This might be a crazy request, but I need you to get me one of those tech guys. One of the conference leaders. Now."

"I'm sorry?"

"Do it now and send them to Room 416."

"Yes, sir."

Nevett turned to him as the manager scurried out of the office. "What are you thinking?"

"Something happened when she checked her email. We need to know what. And we need someone who can figure out what she was doing."

Five minutes later Griffin was sitting across from a man at the small table in his hotel room. "What's your name?"

"Graham."

"Graham, I need you to recover the deleted internet history on this laptop."

The man squirmed in his chair. "Is this even legal?"

"You're doing this for the FBI. Our witness was looking at her email account."

Graham frowned but started clicking on the keyboard. "Looks like there was just one website erased from the history. A Gmail account."

"I need to get into that account."

"I can't—"

Griffin leaned forward. "A young woman could die if you don't."

"But there are rules in place—"

"Just do it."

The man tugged on the edge of his T-shirt, his frown deepening. "Okay, but it's going to take a few minutes."

"Let me know the second you have something."

Griffin started pacing. There were half a dozen officers searching the blocks around the hotel, but he knew Tory had to be long gone. Where?

He needed a distraction while Graham worked. He retraced her movements in his mind. She'd left the living room and gone straight to her bedroom. He opened the door and stepped into the room, feeling the emptiness without her there. She'd left a couple of things on the bed. Her small suitcase and coat were set neatly on the floor. He assumed she had some cash. Wearing her heavier coat would have been too obvious, so she'd left it behind. But why hadn't she just come to him? After all they'd gone through, didn't she trust him?

She did. He knew that, but he also knew she'd do anything to keep her sister safe if that was what they were looking at. But doing this on her own…she never should have done that. They could have come up with a solution to keep them both safe.

Still, it was hard to blame her for what she'd done. Her FBI escort had been hit and now, presumably, Jinx had discovered some kind of leverage on her. She might trust Griffin, but she had every right not to trust the system. If there was a leak somewhere, which he feared there was, she'd simply been protecting what she loved. He just wished they could have found a way together, because if anything happened to her…

Feelings swept through him like a dull knife. Regrets for not anticipating what Jinx would do. Making her feel as if she had to do this on her own when he would have done anything in his power to help her.

Because Caden had been right. He was falling for Tory. There was no denying it. But did that really change anything? He would have risked everything to save Lilly and yet that desire hadn't been enough. And if he ended up losing Tory now… No. He couldn't let his mind go there.

He pushed away the thought, knowing if he was going to save her, he needed to focus on what was going on. He studied the room. The phone book had been pulled out of the desk drawer, and while it lay closed on the desktop, there was a pen set inside it.

And an *X* next to one of the taxi services.

She'd given him a clue.

He quickly dialed the number. "This is Deputy Griffin O'Callaghan from Timber Falls. I'm looking for a young woman who called for a taxi from the Summit Hotel in the past fifteen minutes. I need to know where she was going."

There was a short pause on the line. "I have a call that came through for a pickup a couple blocks from the Summit Hotel, but no drop-off address. I can call the driver and get an address—"

"Deputy O'Callaghan?" the computer tech shouted from the other room.

"Give me a second," Griffin hollered back at Graham, then finished his conversation with the taxi service. "See if you can find out where that taxi went. I'll call you back."

Griffin rushed into the living room. "What have you got?"

"I was able to restore the history. She'd erased it but hadn't logged out of the account."

Griffin sat and pulled the laptop into his lap. There it was. The short email from Jinx.

This isn't over. I have your sister.
Do not involve the police or she is dead.

The words shot through him.

There was also an address.

"Can you tell me what's at that address?" Griffin asked as Agent Nevett walked into the room.

"Just a sec—" Graham said. "Looks like it's a business...an insurance company."

Griffin stared at the screen. He was missing something.

"Send a couple patrol cars to this address," Griffin said to Nevett.

"Do you think she's there?" the agent asked, pulling out his radio.

"I think she was there. But it makes more sense that he sent her there, then had someone pick her up."

Griffin grabbed his phone and put in a call to his boss, Sheriff Jackson.

"I need some information," Griffin said as soon as the man picked up. "You were given copies of the case files about Jinx Ryder, weren't you?"

"Yes…what's going on?"

"Jinx got to Tory."

"How?" the sheriff asked.

"Through an email. He has her sister. I need to know if he owns any property in the area. Any place he might take her."

"I can look through the file, but I'm going to have to call you back. And, Griffin… I suggest we keep this as quiet as we can until we figure out who the leak is."

"I agree."

"I'll see what I can come up with, then plan to meet you there."

Griffin grabbed his key before heading out and down the hall toward the hotel parking lot. Maybe his gut was wrong, but it was worth making sure they didn't miss something. She was out there somewhere, and he had to find her.

He'd just made it to his truck when Sheriff Jackson called him back.

"According to the records I have, Jinx doesn't own anything in the city."

"Then where would he take her? His parents' home, a distant relative, or one of his men. I need something."

There was a long pause before the sheriff spoke again. "I found a piece of property on record that's owned by Jinx's aunt who recently passed away. It's a long shot—"

"Send me the address."

"I just did. I'll be right behind you."

A minute later Griffin jumped into the truck, started the engine and put the address into the GPS. He peeled out of the parking lot and headed east. According to the GPS, the house was twelve miles northeast of town, and Tory was already at least twenty minutes ahead of him.

He knew her well enough to know that she'd do anything it took to save her sister, even if it meant risking her own life in the process. But now that Jinx had them, Griffin knew she'd just put both of their lives on the line.

All he could do now was pray he got there in time.

FIFTEEN

Tory sat next to her sister on a flowered couch in the living room of a house somewhere outside of Denver. Memories continued to flood to the surface. She remembered everything now. Somehow seeing Jinx— and hearing his voice—had been the trigger that had opened up the rest of her memory. She squeezed her eyes shut, but she could still see his face that day. The details of the tan hunting jacket he wore and the mud caked on his boots. She remembered it all.

Jinx shouting orders at his men as he walked toward the edge of the ravine.

The sound of his rifle firing.

The two people he'd killed in front of her.

The horrifying memory that had been there all along and wasn't going away.

He stood in front of them now, the crease across his forehead sharpened by the scowl on his face. A white scar on his neck from a previous fight…a row of tattoos down his arm.

Tory squeezed her sister's hand. "It's going to be okay."

Elizabeth shook her head. "I don't think so—"

"Shut up. Both of you, and just listen. Because let me tell you, I'm tired of all of this. Because of you, I've got every cop and FBI agent in the state after me."

Tory held back her snippy response. She wasn't the one who'd somehow managed to escape a prison transport before kidnapping her and her sister, but it had suddenly become her fault? Her eyes shifted to the door behind him as she searched for a viable way out. She wanted to believe that Griffin was going to walk through the door any minute, but the clue she'd left him had been a long shot. He didn't know where she was. That left her alone, trying to protect her sister from an armed, escaped convict.

Jinx pulled up a wooden chair and sat across from them. "You tried to be so clever by scrubbing your identity online so I wouldn't know you had a sister, but I found her. It wasn't that hard, really. I should have realized that some sheriff deputy wouldn't be enough to motivate you to tell the truth, but your sister…" He leaned forward and ran his thumb down Elizabeth's cheek. "I have a feeling you're going to react differently this time."

Tory bit the inside of her lip while she continued praying God would intervene. "Leave her alone and tell me what you want."

Jinx leaned forward. "You already know what I want. The identity of the other witness. Who was it? Because while the fools I sent after you might have fallen for your amnesia story, I haven't. So here's what's going to happen. There's only one thing I want from you, and if you don't give it to me, your sister dies."

She closed her mouth. Arguing with the man wasn't going to change anything.

So he still didn't know. And he thought she'd made everything up. She had no idea how, but somehow she needed to use that to her advantage.

Tory kept her gaze straight ahead as an idea started to form in her mind. Her anxiety swelled at the thought of taking a risk that might affect her sister. If she went through with this, there would be no turning back. And she already knew what Jinx did to people who crossed him. If it backfired, she was risking both her life and her sister's. But if it worked…

All I wanted to do was what was right, God, and now…now it's not just my life at stake, it's Elizabeth's, as well. I'm not sure I can do this alone…

She kept praying as she looked up at Jinx, searching for the right words to say.

"I'll make a deal with you," she said finally.

"I don't make deals."

"Maybe you'll change your mind when I tell you what it is. You let my sister go and when I have proof she's safe, I'll tell you who was with me that day."

"Like I said…I don't make deals."

"Then I'm sorry. Because you and I both know that there was someone else with me that day—someone that at least one or two people from the Bureau knew about. And if something happens to me, they'll still have another witness. They'll bring that witness in and convince them to testify against you. And trust me, if the second witness knows you killed me…they'll testify."

"You lied before about losing your memory. How do I know you're not lying again?"

Tory wasn't going to argue with him. She just had to convince him that he needed her. And to get what he wanted, Jinx had to agree to send her sister to safety. What happened after that didn't really matter.

She swallowed hard. "Let my sister go and I'll give you what you want."

"Tory, no, you can't do that," her sister said. "I won't leave you here—"

"Shut up, because here's the thing... I didn't get to where I am by making deals with people and feeling sorry for them. You want your sister to live, then you'll do exactly what *I* say. My timing. My rules."

Tory squeezed her sister's hand tighter then drew in a slow breath in an attempt to calm her nerves. "And I'm supposed to trust you? I saw you murder two people without flinching. You shot them then walked away like you'd just done a round of...of target practice. So if you want to know who it is, you'll do things my way."

She could see a glint of desperation in his steely eyes. Jinx might be tough, but he had his vulnerabilities. That was impossible to avoid. And she'd just tapped into one, which gave her an advantage. He was a man who'd spent his life covering all his bases to ensure the Feds couldn't get him by never leaving behind any evidence or witnesses.

She now had him in a place where he needed her.

One of the other men stepped into the room. "Boss, I think we have a problem."

Jinx frowned at the interruption and nodded at the other man. "Take them both upstairs and tie them up."

Tory said nothing, but paid attention to the layout of

the house as the man forced them upstairs, following his boss's orders.

The moment he left the room, she started working on trying to undo the rope. He'd been too distracted and hadn't pulled the ropes tight, which she was going to use to her advantage. And now that they were alone, this might be their only chance. If they could make it out of the house and to the nearest neighbor, maybe they could get help.

"He's not going to do what he said." Elizabeth's chest heaved. "He'll kill us both."

"No, he won't. He needs me."

"Maybe, but if you let me go…once you tell him what he wants to know…he'll kill you."

She was right. Tory knew that. But it didn't matter right now. What mattered was keeping her sister safe and taking this window of opportunity to get them both out of there.

The rope dug into her wrists, but she kept working it. "It will buy us time for Griffin to find us, and that's all that matters."

"Who's Griffin?" Elizabeth asked.

"He's a deputy that was helping me. There are dozens of men looking for Jinx and now for us. They will find us."

"Tory—"

"I'm free. We need to go. Now."

"If we try to escape, they'll kill us both."

Tory reached down and started untying her sister. "It's worth the risk. If we stay here, we're both almost certainly dead."

Her mind formulated a plan as she quickly worked to

undo the knots. She had no idea where her sudden burst of courage had come from, other than a determination to ensure Jinx and his men didn't win. And knowing that this was what Griffin would do if he were in her place. She couldn't stop doing everything in her power to get them both out alive.

"One more second…" She tugged on the end of one of the ropes until it slipped out. Elizabeth was free. "Let's go."

"Where?"

Tory hurried to the window and looked out. The drop made an escape from this room impossible.

"Follow me."

Not only had she studied the layout of the two-story house, she'd taken in as many details of the property as possible when she'd arrived with Jinx's men. The property itself was expansive, surrounded at least in part by a fence and filled with trees. They were now on the second floor of a large house, at the end of the hall. She'd only seen one staircase, but there might be another window they could use as an escape in one of the other rooms.

Tory grabbed Elizabeth's hand and pulled her to the door, listening for movement before she slowly opened it. She could hear voices coming from downstairs. She had no idea what the problem was, but at least Jinx was occupied for the moment.

A second later footsteps pounded up the stairs in front of them.

"Tory—"

"We need to hide. Now."

Tory pulled her sister through the closest doorway,

knowing there was really no place to hide in the house where Jinx and his men wouldn't eventually find them. They would know that she and her sister couldn't have gone far. All they needed to do was a systematic search of the house, which meant her only option at the moment was to buy them time. Time enough for Griffin to find her, which she knew he would. But how long was that going to take? It was a question she couldn't answer.

Guilt swept through her as she shut the bedroom door behind her. She regretted not simply going to Griffin and telling him what had happened, but she'd been too scared that Jinx would follow through with his threats if she hadn't done exactly what he'd said.

All she'd ever wanted was to protect her sister.

"They're coming, Tory."

"I know."

She could hear the panic in her sister's voice as she studied the room they'd walked into. At the moment fear was the enemy. Just like in the emergency room, she needed to keep her focus despite everything that was going on around her and not let herself be pulled in by the fear.

Inhaling a calming breath, she glanced around the room. Like what she'd seen of the rest of the large house, it was nicely furnished with a queen-size bed, end tables, a dresser, a bookshelf and a comfy chair. There was nowhere to hide beyond the closet or under the bed. They needed more than just a hiding place. They had to get away from this house.

Tory quickly crossed the room, stopping at the window, where she found the advantage they needed. While there'd been no easy escape from the other room, they should be able to make it to the ground from this one. They could climb down to the balcony that ended on the edge of the next room, about two feet from the window where she stood. Once they made it to the ground, they'd still have to find a way off the property, but for now she was simply going to focus on getting herself and her sister out of the house.

"We're going out the window, Elizabeth."

Her sister tugged at her arm. "There's no time. They're coming now."

Tory froze for a second as footsteps pounded down the hall toward their location, passed the room they were in and then stopped. A door slammed open. Someone had just discovered they were gone. She made a rapid decision and motioned for her sister to slide under the bed. She quickly pulled open the window before searching the room for a weapon. She grabbed a heavy bookend from the bookshelf and then scrambled under the bed with her sister.

The space beneath the bed was tight, but she refused to imagine what would happen if Jinx found them. Instead she started praying. Praying that the men wouldn't find them. That Griffin would find them first and that she'd know what to do in the meantime.

She drew in a slow breath while her heart pounded in her ears. She'd tried to convince Elizabeth that Griffin would save them, but she knew the truth. She was fooling herself if she thought she could win this cat-and-mouse game against Jinx and his men. Or ignore what they would do if they found her now. No one, not even Griffin, knew where they were.

"Stay still," she said. "We're going to be okay."

Tory had tried to put a measure of confidence into her voice, but she was facing the same doubts. She was on her own now and it wasn't just her life hanging in the balance. She couldn't let anything happen to Elizabeth, but she'd seen Jinx murder two people. It was the reason she was here.

Please, God... We're out of options.

She stared at the bottom of the doorframe. Not knowing what was happening on the other side of that door had her adrenaline pulsing through her. She considered trying to make the escape out the window now, but she knew that whoever was out there could step into the room at any moment. It wasn't worth the risk.

The sound of the door opening sent her heart racing even faster. A moment later footsteps thumped against the wood flooring. Someone walked across the room, stopping on the thick rug at the end of the bed. They lay motionless.

It wasn't Jinx. She could tell by the boots that it was the man who'd brought them up here and restrained them. Jinx must have sent him upstairs to get them. Judging by the fact that he hadn't yet called for reinforcements when he'd discovered they were gone, she knew why. If they were missing, he was the one who'd be held responsible. And knowing what Jinx had already done to those who crossed him in any way, the man had to be in a panic.

Elizabeth's fingers squeezed her hand tighter.

Tory pressed her lips together, determined not to move or make a sound. Their lives depended on him not discovering they were in the room.

He made a slow circle, as if trying to figure out where

they might have gone. She tried to puzzle out his thought processes. He'd seen the empty room where he'd left them and knew he would have seen them on the stairs if they'd tried to escape that way. That meant he knew that the only other escape route was through the window.

He walked toward the window, distracted as she'd hoped he'd be. He'd likely noticed the cold draft of air coming into the room and was wondering why the window was open. She took in a breath, trying to slow her breathing. Trying to figure out what she was going to do if he didn't come to the conclusion she hoped for and decided to look under the bed. For a few seconds they might have an advantage with two against one, but she had to assume he was armed. On top of that, she knew he could also call for Jinx and the other men for backup.

She heard the window creak open a few more inches then stop. He was looking outside. Trying to figure out where they'd gone. She continued her prayer as the man turned back toward the bed and then paused again. He was going through the scenario in his head, trying to decide what to do. Another few seconds passed. She counted them in her head. One…two…three….

He stomped across the room, toward the door to the hall, then left. Tory let out a whoosh of air as the door slammed behind him. Her plan had worked. He'd believed that they'd escaped through the window and onto the balcony. That meant they'd start searching the grounds. In the meantime she needed to find a phone where she could call 9-1-1. And maybe keys to a car.

Voices rumbled from downstairs as the men shouted at each other. Jinx, no doubt, had just learned what had happened. Their prisoners had escaped and, knowing Jinx, someone was going to pay. But there was no time to run through the possible scenarios in her mind or the long list of what-ifs that kept trying to crowd her thoughts.

"We need to go now," she said, motioning for her sister to follow her. But Elizabeth remained frozen beneath the bed. "Elizabeth…"

"I can't."

"We need to find a phone and a way out of here, which means we have to go now."

Elizabeth still didn't move.

"They think we left through the window," Tory said. "They're going to start searching the grounds."

"No. They're going to find us."

"Not if we're smarter. Push back the fear, because I need you to come with me."

Something must have clicked in her sister's mind. She nodded and then crawled out from under the bed, a new glint of determination in her eyes.

"We can do this. We just have to be smarter than they are."

"Okay." Elizabeth paused. "Do you hear them?"

Tory shook her head. The house was quiet. Eerily quiet. A dog barked, but she wasn't sure if it was on the grounds surrounding the house or in a neighboring home. They needed to get downstairs where there should be a phone, but first she crossed the room and stood in the shadow of the window. She'd been right. She could see the three men moving away from the front of the house. They were spreading out on the large plot of land, clearly determined to search until they found Tory and Elizabeth.

SIXTEEN

Griffin sped down the two-lane road that headed out of the city, toward the address his boss had given him, praying his instincts were right. Because if he was wrong, he was looking at another dead end. The officers had checked the address Jinx had told Tory to go to, but there had been no sign of her there. Something that didn't surprise him. He gripped the steering wheel, angry that Jinx had somehow won another round. Tory had been safe—or at least that's what he'd thought—but Jinx had still managed to get through to her.

He punched the button on his steering wheel and used the voice-command option to call Sheriff Jackson.

"How far out are you?" he asked, dispensing with formalities.

"We're about ten minutes behind you."

"Good," Griffin said. He wasn't willing to take any chances that something went wrong with this rescue. It was time to put an end to it all.

"I know you're worried about her," Sheriff Jackson said, "but you need to wait for backup before you go charging in there."

"I agree, but ten minutes might be too late."

"Then go ahead and survey the situation and find out what we're walking into, but don't do anything that could risk your life or hers, Griffin."

"I won't."

Because he wasn't going to let anything happen to her. He couldn't. Not after everything they'd been through together. He ended the call and stepped on the gas. His motivation scared him. He'd only known her for a few days and yet, somehow, he knew he'd never be the same again.

His mind shifted momentarily to Lilly. Was she the underlying factor to what he was really feeling? His chance to redeem himself? He still remembered every detail leading up to the moment he'd found out she was dead, every chance he'd had to ask just one more question that could have in turn changed the circumstances and saved her life.

But Lilly was dead and nothing was going to change that fact. This was not redemption; it was simply another life on the line. One he was determined to save, because that was who he was.

He stopped at the end of the long drive leading into the gated property, completely focused now on the task at hand—despite the fact that he had nothing more than a basic plan in mind with backup still minutes behind him. The two-story house sat back from the road, the property enclosed by an iron gate that surrounded the large slice of land for as far as he could see. From his vantage point, he couldn't spot any security cameras, but that didn't mean they weren't there. He also knew that Jinx wouldn't be there alone and that he and his men would all be armed.

Griffin's heart pounded as he exited his truck, jumped the security gate and slipped down into the yard, his boots crunching against the gravel drive. He moved into the shadows of the tree line, hoping to get the information Sheriff Jackson had asked for. How many men were they up against? Where were the girls being held? These were the questions he had to answer, but in the process, he couldn't take a chance and give away his approach.

He started across the yard and heard men's voices. It sounded like they were at the back of the house, but from where he was, he couldn't see them. He continued toward the house, approaching cautiously. Another dozen yards and he'd be on the south side of the house, where he could tell there was a door.

Hearing rustling in the bushes ahead of him, he held out his weapon. A Doberman approached from the left, clearly aware that someone had just breached the property. Its ears were up and forward as the dog's stare pierced straight through him.

You've got to be kidding me.

Griffin quickly ran through his options. Going back to the fence where he'd come over wasn't an option. He was too far away now. The house was in front of him, but there was no way he was going to be able to simply run in through the front door. That left the giant oak tree in front of him. It had branches with access to the roof. If he could climb high enough, he might be able to avoid getting caught.

He didn't take time to second-guess his decision.

The dog started barking as it ran toward him. Griffin holstered his weapon and quickly scrambled up the tree. The higher branches were narrower than he would have liked and swayed slightly with his weight, but if he hurried and timed it just right, he could make it onto the roof.

The dog continued barking at the foot of the tree. It wouldn't be long until someone noticed. He needed to ensure he was out of sight by the time they arrived, which probably gave him five, maybe ten, seconds at the most.

He shimmied his way along the branches toward the roof, thankful for all his years on the ranch climbing trees and building tree houses. His father had always called him Mowgli from *The Jungle Book* because of his hunting and tracking skills. Now he just needed to use them to save Tory and her sister.

Someone shouted from below as Griffin jumped onto the slick tiled roof then scrambled up to the crest and onto the other side. A second man responded. Griffin held his breath, bracing himself to make sure he didn't fall. But if they came around to this side of the house, they'd see him. He needed a better place to hide.

He pulled himself back, out of view, praying they didn't hear the scuffling on the roof. He could smell the musty scent of cigarette smoke as two men—neither of which he recognized—ran around the corner. The dog barked louder at the foot of the tree. One of them shouted out a command and then all was quiet.

One of the men held back the dog. "Probably just one of the neighbors' cats."

"Or it was them."

"Are you sure she left through that window?"

"The window was open…they were gone…"

"Maybe that's what she wanted you to think, but there isn't enough snow to show footprints."

"Well, if they're not out here, they have to still be in the house."

"Where's Jinx?"

"Still searching down by the pond."

The men headed back to the house, making any more of their conversation impossible for Griffin to hear. But he'd heard enough. Tory and her sister had managed to escape. What he didn't know was where they were. The two men believed they were still inside the house…

Griffin glanced below him. There was a balcony he assumed led to one of the rooms on the second floor. If he could find an unlocked window…reach them first…

His boots began to slide on the icy roof. He grabbed onto a metal vent and managed to stop himself from falling. His fingers were almost frozen, but he ignored the discomfort. He needed to get inside the house, do a quick search and find out if Tory was still inside. He moved down to the gutter, jumped onto the balcony and found an open window. Another ten seconds and he was inside the house. The sheriff would be here in four to five minutes. His job now was to make sure he found Tory before Jinx did.

The men's voices grew louder as they came toward the house. Tory and her sister had unsuccessfully searched the downstairs for a phone, but not being able to call for help wasn't the worst thing they were facing. They were trapped. Her plan had been to escape the house, but now not only were the men outside scouring the property, they also had a guard dog. Elizabeth's anxious expression reflected her own fears. She wasn't sure how much longer they could evade Jinx and the other men. And when they were found this time, he wasn't going to listen to her excuses. Jinx would probably just kill them.

Tory squeezed her fingers around Elizabeth's hands. "We need to go back upstairs."

They hurried up to the second floor. There had to be another place to hide. She'd seen the entrance to an attic at the end of the hallway, but there wasn't time to pull down a ladder and get up there.

She heard movement in the bedroom ahead of them and felt the panic ensue. Had one of them come through the window she'd left open?

She squeezed her sister's hand tighter as a man stepped out of one of the bedrooms in front of them.

"Griffin?" Her heart pounded at the sight of his familiar form. "You found us."

He pulled her into his arms, hesitated, then leaned down and kissed her firmly on the lips. Her heart pounded at his nearness as she automatically responded to him. In any other situation, she could see herself exploring what she was feeling, but right now she couldn't get her heart involved. There was too much at stake.

"I'm sorry." He pulled away from her. "I don't know what I was thinking... I was just so worried I wouldn't get here in time. So worried about you. About both of you. Are you okay?"

"Now that you're here, I am. Griffin, this is my sister, Elizabeth."

He nodded. "I read Jinx's email and, long story short, managed to figure out where he'd brought you. I'm just relieved you're both safe."

Tory tried to stomp down the wave of guilt that rose in her. She might have done what she'd thought she'd had to do, but she should have trusted him. "They threatened to kill Elizabeth if I didn't come alone. I didn't know what to do."

"You did what you had to do to protect her." His glance shifted to Elizabeth. "Because you're the other witness, aren't you?"

Elizabeth nodded.

"I remember most of what happened that day." Tory took in a deep breath, wishing she could erase the flood of elusive memories that had finally surfaced. "I tried to make a deal with him. Told him to let her go and I'd take him to the other witness."

"And somehow you managed to escape?"

"Yes. They're on their way back into the house, leaving us trapped."

"I saw two outside and Jinx is out there, as well. Are there any more?"

"Far as I know, that's all."

He squeezed her hand. "Backup is on the way and these guys aren't going to get away with what they did."

"What are our options in the meantime?"

"Avoiding confrontation, which means I need a place to hide the two of you."

They slipped down the hallway, listening for signs that anyone else was still in the house, but she didn't like the slim chance of them getting out alive. It might be three against three, but Griffin was the only one of them that was armed, leaving them at a huge disadvantage.

A floorboard creaked downstairs.

"They're back inside," Tory said.

Griffin nodded as they passed a bathroom door. "Go in here and stay back, away from the door."

"You can't do this on your own, Griffin—"

"Trust me." He reached into his pocket and gave her his pepper spray. "Use it if you need it, but we have the advantage. They don't know I'm here."

There was no time to come up with a plan, but the element of surprise turned out to be exactly what he needed.

Griffin took the first man down in two sharp punches and then quickly pulled his limp body into the bathroom. With Tory's help, they hoisted him into the tub and Elizabeth shoved a washcloth into his mouth to keep him silent once he came to.

"I know where some rope is." Tory scurried out of the room, returning seconds later with enough rope to secure him and at least one more.

One down. Two to go.

A second man ran up the stairs, clearly angry as he shouted something at his downed partner. Griffin didn't give him time to react. His elbow struck the man's jawbone, knocking him onto the carpet. Griffin let out a sharp huff of relief.

Two down without firing a bullet.

He finished confirming the men were securely tied, knowing this wasn't over. Tory stood beside him, looking tired, but there was still a fight in her eyes. Her loss of memory was probably the only thing that had kept them alive, and now that she remembered…

Griffin's jaw clenched. He wasn't even going to try to imagine what might have happened if he hadn't managed to find her. And that kiss… He didn't know what he'd been thinking, but the thought of losing her terrified him.

He spoke into his radio. "Jackson, how far out are you?"

"A minute…two at the most."

Griffin frowned. He wasn't sure they had two minutes.

"Where are you?"

"Upstairs with the women and two of the men."

"Try to hold off a confrontation with Jinx until we get there."

"I'll try, but even if I don't do anything, I can guarantee he's going to come to us."

That was inevitable.

The stairs at the end of the hallway creaked.

He'd been right. Jinx was coming.

Griffin motioned for Tory and her sister to stay in the bathroom, guarding the men. Then he stood waiting in the recessed doorway, senses on alert and ready to defend them if necessary.

Jinx started clearing the rooms. "Robert! Carl! What's going on up here?"

While Griffin had planned to do his best to wait for backup, he knew Jinx wasn't going down without a fight, and he had to keep Tory and her sister out of the line of fire.

"Police!" Griffin stepped into the hallway, recognizing the man from his mug shot. "Put the gun on the floor, then raise your hands in the air!"

Jinx frowned, clearly taken aback by Griffin's presence. "You just can't stay out of this, can you?"

"This never should have happened."

"Oh, but it did. And if you think you're going to just walk out of here, you're wrong."

"Your men have been subdued, which means it's just you and me now. There's nowhere to go, Jinx. This is over."

"Oh, it's far from over. Where is she?"

"It doesn't matter where she is. You're done using her."

"You're wrong. I've arranged for a way out of the country. The good thing for you is that I'll disappear. The unfortunate thing is that you won't get to enjoy it. All I have to do is take you down and she and her sister will come with me as leverage to ensure I get out of here without any issues."

"Put the gun down, Jinx, because as much as you'd like to think what you just said is true, none of that is going to happen," Griffin said, moving back against the recessed door. "Backup will be here within the next minute. I've got your men secured, which means you'll be outmanned and outgunned."

Jinx's gun went off and slammed a bullet into the doorframe behind Griffin. Griffin returned fire, hitting his mark. But before Griffin could move toward the injured man, Jinx fired off a second round. Griffin felt the impact as the bullet ripped through his leg. A moment later he collapsed to the floor.

SEVENTEEN

Tory heard the gunshots in the hallway, followed by an eerie silence. Panic welled inside her. She cracked open the door, terrified as to what she was about to find. Jinx was motionless on the ground a dozen feet from where Griffin lay, a pool of blood beginning to gather beneath him. She needed to move quickly. This was no graze.

Griffin grabbed her arm. "Get back into the bathroom until backup comes."

She ignored his orders. "Elizabeth, help me pull him into the bathroom."

They moved Griffin out of the doorway, careful not to injure him further.

"Griffin, can you still hear me?"

"Yeah. I… I think I'm okay."

"You're not okay. You've got a bullet in your leg. We have to get you to a hospital." Tory glanced down the hall where Jinx was trying to sit up, then quickly shut the door and locked it.

As long as Jinx was alive, he was going to come after them, but she couldn't worry about him for the moment. Instead she quickly assessed Griffin's wound, finding both the entry and exit. But it was bleeding too much. She needed to elevate his leg then create a makeshift pressure bandage to stop the bleeding.

God, please...this can't be happening. Not after everything else we've gotten through...

They'd managed to escape and now lay trapped in the upstairs of some old house with a murderer after them.

It couldn't end this way.

Elizabeth hovered above her as she worked. "How bad is it?"

Tory ripped away the fabric around the wound and examined it. "Bad. I have to find a way to control the bleeding."

"What do you need from me?"

"Are the other men still secure?"

Elizabeth glanced behind her. "They're not going anywhere."

"Then look in the cabinets and get me some towels."

A moment later Elizabeth handed her a stack of washcloths. "How are we going to get out of here with Jinx in the way?"

Sirens sounded in the background. Maybe there was a way out of this, after all.

"With help, hopefully." Tory focused back on Griffin. "You're going to be fine, but I need you to stay awake."

"Tory... If he comes after you..."

"Forget about Jinx for the moment."

But that was impossible.

"I know he's injured," Jinx's voice shouted from the hallway. "But you're not going anywhere until I'm out of here."

She checked Griffin's pulse, her own heart beating rapidly, worried he would go into shock.

"Don't go out there," Griffin said.

"I'm not, but we need to end this," she said, picking up his weapon.

"Do you know how to shoot a gun?"

"I've gone to the gun range a few times."

"We've got three bullets. If I pass out—"

"You're not going to pass out. Just hold on, Griffin, please… Help is coming."

She quickly went through their options. Barricading themselves had simply meant delaying the inevitable. Because while Jinx might be injured, if he came in after them, they had to be ready.

She motioned at her sister. "Hold this as tight as you can against the wound, while I move the cabinet against the wall."

Tory scrambled to push the furniture, but it was too late. Jinx smashed into the door, trying to break it open. She pressed on it with all of her weight, but she wasn't strong enough. Seconds later it slammed open, almost knocking her off balance.

She stepped back, gripping Griffin's weapon with two hands and holding it out in front of her in a face-off with Jinx.

"Put the gun down, Tory."

She stood her ground, refusing to flinch at his command. The few times she'd gone to the range had taught her the basic mechanics of firing a gun. Shooting another person—even in self-defense—terrified her, but if she had to do it to save Griffin and Elizabeth, she knew she would.

"Don't take another step forward," she said, holding her hands steady.

"Or what? You'll shoot me?" He leaned against the doorframe, a stain of red blood on his side as he kept his gun aimed at her. "You don't have it in you."

"Don't be so sure. It might surprise you what a person can do when the people they love are threatened."

"Maybe, but by the time you shoot me, I'll have already taken down you and your sister and finished off your boyfriend there."

"Leave them out of this. This is between you and me."

"You're stronger than I thought, but in the end it doesn't matter. I always win. And if you choose the hard way, you'll be the one who pays."

"In case you hadn't noticed, the sheriff and the FBI have arrived."

Jinx was trying to take charge of the situation. Trying to intimidate her. But he was weakening from the loss of blood. She could see it in his eyes. The red stain was spreading. Sweat beaded above his forehead. And while adrenaline might be pumping at the moment and keeping him going, it wouldn't be long until he collapsed. She just had to somehow find a way to buy them all time until that happened, without anyone else getting shot.

Jinx motioned behind her. "Get them on the radio, so I can tell them exactly what's going to happen. If not, all three of you are going to die."

What terrified her was that every minute that passed was another minute Griffin wasn't getting the medical help he needed. But there was an even bigger problem at the moment. Even if she did get a shot off and hit her target, Jinx could easily take one or more of them down in the same amount of time.

"Do what I said. Now!" he ordered.

Not moving, she addressed her sister. "Elizabeth, slide the radio next to me and make the call."

She waited a few seconds for Elizabeth to comply.

"This is Tory Faraday," she said once someone answered. "Jinx is here. He's armed and making demands."

"Tory, this is Sheriff Jackson. Is anyone hurt?"

"Griffin was shot."

"How bad is he?"

"He was shot in the leg. He's losing a lot of blood and needs medical attention immediately."

"What kinds of demands?" the sheriff asked.

Tory took a deep breath and caught Jinx's gaze. "Tell them what you want."

"You've got one minute to get your people off my property. In the meantime, I'll be taking a hostage with me, so if I were you, I wouldn't interfere."

"Can you tell me where you are?"

"In the upstairs bathroom—" Tory started to say.

"Don't answer that!"

Tory could hear voices in the background before the radio went silent.

She still had her finger on the trigger when a shot rang out. Jinx slumped to the ground in the doorway in front of her. A second later Tory felt her knees buckle as a uniformed deputy stepped into the room with the paramedics right behind him. She blinked back the terror. She couldn't panic now.

"There are two shooting victims," she said. "Both patients are conscious, or at least they were before you shot him. Deputy O'Callaghan has a through-and-through to the leg, his heart rate is a hundred and twenty. He has previous injuries to his rib cage and a graze from a bullet to his forearm from a couple days ago. The other men that were with Jinx are secured the bathtub."

The officer stopped, as if trying to take in what she was saying. "Are you okay, ma'am?"

Tory nodded but felt as if she were about to pass out.

"Both of you?"

Elizabeth grabbed Tory's arm and nodded. "We're fine."

"There are two ambulances here. We'll get both men out right away."

"I'm a nurse, I can help."

"You've done everything you need to for the moment." He put a hand on her shoulder. "You're a victim, too, ma'am, and we're going to want both of you to be checked out, as well."

"He's going into shock—"

"I'll make sure he's okay."

She nodded as the paramedics went to work, but his words did little to calm her fears. All she could do now was pray that it wasn't too late for Griffin.

Tory headed down the tiled hall of the hospital. The last week had proved to be physically exhausting as well as emotional as the last few pieces of her memory managed to come back. The FBI had been able to track down most of Jinx's men. He was now sitting in isolation in a prison cell. The one positive thing that had come out of this mess.

She'd planned to go home at the beginning of the week, once she knew Griffin was going to be okay, but somehow Elizabeth had convinced her she needed a few more days of rest before they left.

Visiting Griffin in the hospital every day had seemed like the perfect excuse to see him, and she'd enjoyed her time with him. They'd watched movies, played card games and twice she'd snuck in something from the local diner for him. They'd talked until the nurses kicked her out. From their time together, she'd discovered she loved his laugh, his sense of humor and, even more, his company.

She told herself the only reason she kept coming by was that she owed him. He'd taken a bullet for her—twice—and she couldn't take that for granted. But she knew it was more than that. Not only did he know how to make her laugh, she felt comfortable with him and somehow couldn't imagine not having him in her life.

Every morning for the past few days, she'd woken up excited to see him, but there was something still holding her back from letting him past the wall she'd erected around her heart. She knew now that there was no one waiting for her back home. No boyfriend or fiancé who'd held a piece of her heart or had been worried about her while she'd been out in the storm, running for her life.

And maybe that in itself was the problem. Everything she *could* remember now.

Like promising her parents she'd take care of Elizabeth if anything happened to them and then, at twenty-one, watching their caskets being lowered into the ground. She'd taken extra shifts at the hospital where she'd just started working, determined to keep Elizabeth in college and a roof over their heads. There had simply never been time for a relationship. Nothing had really changed; staying in Timber Falls was only going to make things worse.

Griffin was standing by the window, looking out at the mountains, when she stepped into his room.

"Well…look at that," she said, struggling to put aside her troubled thoughts for the moment. "You finally decided to get out of bed."

He smiled back at her. "Very funny."

"You look good. Color's back in your cheeks, your bruises are fading more every day…"

"I feel good. The physical therapy is paying off and I finally feel like my strength is coming back."

"I brought a crossword puzzle book, thinking you needed something a bit more challenging, but you might not need me to entertain you anymore."

"I wouldn't say that, though you're probably just sick of bad hospital jokes and my leftover Jell-O."

Tory let out a slow laugh. "Both of those are things I'm definitely going to miss. What's the doctor saying?"

"He's pleased with my progress and said it's time I went home. I'm hoping later today once they get all the paperwork finished."

"Hospitals are notoriously slow with their paperwork. Once you're out, you're still going to have to be careful with what you do. Make sure you continue with the physical therapy to get your strength and range of motion back. You want to be able to get back to work."

"Yes, ma'am. I'll definitely do all of that. Thankfully, the doctor has assured me that I should get back my full range of motion, though I'm going to miss having such a good nurse taking care of me."

Griffin's words sliced through her. Because now that he was going home, she had no more excuses to stay.

"I'm glad to hear you're going home, though I have a feeling you might not be quite so agreeable when the FBI asks you to help them with a case again."

"They're not letting me go back to work for a while, but you're right. Though I have a feeling another case with them would never be quite the same." His gaze seemed to pierce right through her. "I might get roped into taking care of some old, balding man."

She shot him a smile. "Do you have something against bald men?"

"Not at all. But there is something about taking a bullet for a beautiful woman in distress that makes a better story."

Tory's heart stirred at his words. She never should have let her emotions get so tangled. She had no real ties to him or his family, but what she did have was a life back in Santa Fe where friends and coworkers were expecting her to return. Besides, while Griffin might be smart, charming and undeniably handsome, they both knew the reality. Nothing was ever going to happen between them. She'd only managed to drag out the inevitable by staying in Timber Falls as long as she had. She'd go back to work and, before long, he'd forget about her.

She just wasn't sure she could say the same. She'd never forget him.

"You okay?" he asked.

"Yeah, I'm good. And... I'm sorry but, unfortunately,

I can't stay. I promised my sister I'd meet her for lunch. I just thought I'd drop this by on the way."

Griffin glanced at the clock. "It's just ten."

"I know, but I need to run a couple of errands before meeting her."

Tory set the crossword puzzle book down on the bed and forced a smile. She was making excuses. She didn't have to go, but the more time she spent with him, the harder it was going to be for her heart to leave.

"Are you sure you can't stay for a little bit?" he asked.

"Yeah. I'm sorry—" she took two steps backward toward the door "—but I'll try to see you before I leave to say goodbye."

"Before you leave?"

"I wanted to stay long enough to make sure you were going to be okay, and now that you're going home…"

She caught the disappointment in Griffin's eyes and forced herself not to turn away.

"I guess… I hoped you'd stay longer," he said.

"Elizabeth and I have jobs, and my vacation time is about all used up."

She tried to read his expression. Did he know she had to make excuses just to try to untangle her heart from those eyes that seemed to stare right through her?

"Before you go…" He turned away from her and grabbed something from the side of the bed. "Thanks to the internet and two-day delivery service, I have something for you."

"A present? You didn't have to buy me anything."

"It's a bit of a tradition for our family." He handed her the box then waited for her to open it.

"Wow…" She pulled out a gold-covered aspen leaf. "It's beautiful."

"It's a Christmas ornament and, while I'm sure there are lots of things you'd like to forget about your time here, I hope it will remind you of the good moments."

"Most of what happened over the past few days, I want to forget, but there are other things I will miss."

"Like?"

"Like your family, for starters. They've been amazing. And the ranch… I honestly don't think I've ever seen such a beautiful place. The trees, the mountains and the snow in the morning sun… I won't forget. Ever. Christmas in the mountains is unforgettable."

He sat on the edge of the bed. "There was something else I was hoping might be hard for you to leave behind. Or rather, someone else."

He shot her the smile that managed to melt the edges of her heart. The smile that made her want to open up for the first time in so long.

"You know I'm going to miss you," she said. "You saved my life. You're my hero."

He nodded but she knew she'd answered wrong.

"I hope you miss me, because I know I'm going to miss you, Tory." He caught her gaze and hesitated before continuing. "But not just because you feel indebted to me. What if I told you I didn't want you to go?"

Her breath caught at his words. She knew what he was implying, but that was a place she couldn't afford to go.

"Griffin, I know we've been through a lot together, and I can't deny that there is connection between us." She blinked back the tears, hating the wave of emotion she couldn't control. "But I have a life back in Santa Fe and you have one in Timber Falls. And even though I love it here, I need to be there for my sister. She's my responsibility. And, honestly…honestly, there's just too much here I want to forget."

His jaw tensed. "I guess I thought if you stayed longer, we could see what might happen between us."

"Griffin—"

"You don't have to make a decision right now. Just… just think about it."

"I'm sorry. It's time for me to go home. I have responsibilities. A job. And my sister…she needs me." She tried to swallow the lump in her throat. "Let me know when you're finally discharged, and in the meantime if you need anything…"

Tory started toward the door, the tears welling in her eyes. Everything that had happened over the past couple of weeks had taken its toll; dragging things out here any longer than she already had wasn't wise. She'd allowed her heart to get involved, then let her sister talk her into staying longer, something she never should have done.

"Tory?"

She turned around in the doorway. "Yeah?"

"Thank you. For sticking around as long as you did. I wish you could stay, but I do understand."

She nodded, knowing if she tried to say anything else, she'd lose it.

Griffin had stolen a piece of her heart and she wasn't sure she wanted it back.

EIGHTEEN

Tory pulled a stack of folded shirts out of the hotel dresser drawer, wondering why she'd bothered to unpack when she'd only planned to stay a few days. There was something psychological about unpacking her bags no matter where she was that made her feel more…settled. Getting her memory back had helped, as well. Instead of having to claw her way through a maze of foggy memories, they were all—for the most part—back in their places and had given her back the life she'd temporarily forgotten. She'd been reminded that she had a home and friends to go back to, which made her grateful for what she had.

But if that were true, then why did her heart feel so empty?

She pushed away the rambling thoughts as the door to her room flew open.

"Elizabeth!" She dropped the shirts into the suitcase. "You're back early."

"Why are you packing?"

"Because we decided this morning that we're leaving tomorrow. It's been a week. It's time."

Elizabeth plopped down on the armchair next to the bay window and started pulling off her boots. "I was thinking about staying a couple more days. The weather's perfect for skiing and there's supposed to be fresh powder overnight."

Tory grabbed a dress off the hanger and started folding it. "Some of us have jobs and commitments."

"You're going to miss him, aren't you? Deputy O'Callaghan."

Tory frowned at the question. "Of course. I owe him a lot. He saved my life."

"He saved both our lives, except he isn't in love with me."

Why did being around her sister sometimes feel like she was back in college? "He's not in love with me, either."

"Are you sure about that?"

"Of course."

But that wasn't completely honest. She wasn't sure about anything anymore.

Tory put the last of her clothes into her suitcase, then reached into the top of the dresser and picked up the gold aspen leaf Griffin had given her. She held it up to the window and watched it shimmer in the sunlight.

Elizabeth came to sit in front of her on the bed. "What's going on, Tory?"

"Nothing. I'm just a little tired."

"That's hardly surprising. You've been through a lot. But something tells me that's not all that's going on."

"What do you mean?"

"What do I mean? You saw him this morning, didn't you?"

"Yeah. He…he's going home. But I'm not sure what that matters. It reminded me that it really is time for us to leave, as well."

"What did he say to you?"

"About?"

Elizabeth let out a sharp huff of air and rolled her eyes. "The two of you, of course."

Tory hesitated before answering. "Nothing important."

"Really? Why is it that talking to you is like pulling teeth? Can't you just admit you have feelings for him? Because something tells me what he said was very important. He's in love with you, and I'm pretty sure you feel the same way."

Tory shook her head. "He's not in love with me, for starters. I barely know him. And second, I'm going home, so I can be there for you." She fought back the unwanted tears. "It's time to go home, Elizabeth."

"First of all, I love and appreciate everything you've done for me. I truly do. But I'm twenty-two years old. I can take care of myself."

"I know, but I want to be there for you. Over the past couple of weeks, it was as if I'd lost everything. Finding it again has been a reminder to me of how important family and friends are. I'm ready to go back and start working again. Just like I used to. I don't want what happened here to change me."

"You mean what happened with Jinx."

Tory tried to blink back the tears and sat beside her sister. "I'm sorry."

Her sister wrapped her arm around her shoulder and pulled her tight. "You have nothing to be sorry about, but stop denying that what happened has changed you. You risked everything to keep me safe, had a criminal try to kill you, lost your memory in the process… You've changed, but for better. So be gracious to yourself and give yourself time to heal."

Tory let out a soft snort. "Since when did you get to be so wise?"

"I learned it all from you." Elizabeth laughed. "But I need you to listen to me. You've spent your entire life taking care of me. It's time you lived your own life. And you say you don't know him, but I've seen the two of you together. There's this connection that doesn't come around every day. I just… I think you should give him a chance."

Tory set down the leaf she'd been holding. "Forget it. I don't need a matchmaker. I have everything I need in my life. You, my friends, my church home—"

Elizabeth stood and went to the window, her hands clasped behind her. "What if I told you I got a job in Minneapolis?"

"Minneapolis?" Tory didn't even try to mask the surprise in her voice.

Elizabeth turned back around. "I think I want to take it."

Somehow Tory had assumed they'd go back to how things had been. "When did this happen?"

"I got the offer right before you left to testify. I didn't want to stress you any more than you already were, so I didn't tell you. At the time I thought we'd work it out as soon as you were home. They want me to start right after the new year."

"Moving to a new city with a new job is huge." She

crossed the room and gave her sister a hug. "I'm so proud of you and not surprised at all. I guess I just... didn't imagine losing you so soon."

"You're not losing me. We can still get together for birthdays and Christmases and vacations."

Tory bit her lip. She shouldn't be surprised. Elizabeth had grown up, but that didn't mean her leaving wasn't going to create a hole in Tory's heart.

"I know this is what you've worked so hard for," Tory said, moving back to her suitcase, "and you know I'd never stand in your way."

"It would be easier for me to leave if I didn't have to worry about you. If you had someone who could take care of you."

"Now you need to stop." She began rearranging the shirts in her suitcase. "I'll be fine. Even without you living close, I'll have my job, my house, and thankfully my memory. But I'll still miss you. If it's the right job, you need to take it."

"I appreciate that." Elizabeth picked up the gold leaf. "Why don't you at least give him a chance? Find out if he's really the one? Because if you walk away and don't ever know what could have happened... Griffin is different. I can tell by the way he looks at you and your voice when you talk about him. Tory, if you leave now, I really think you're going to regret it."

If I leave now, I'll regret it.

Her stomach clenched.

She'd regret it because she loved him.

The thought pierced through her, leaving its mark in the center of her heart. She was losing it. Seriously. How could she love him? They'd been thrown together in some high-profile case with the FBI and state law enforcement involved. She'd been kidnapped, he'd been shot...that wasn't exactly real life. And while she couldn't deny the bond she felt with him, it wasn't love.

Was it?

Then why did she feel as if she'd known him forever?

Griffin O'Callaghan had rescued her physically, but he'd also somehow managed to find a way to rescue her heart.

She sat on the bed. "He asked me to stay. Wanted to give us a chance to see if something might develop between us."

"Are you serious? I was right! I knew it!"

Tory nodded.

"And you actually turned him down?"

"Because it all seems so...complicated. I can't just leave my life for a guy I hardly know."

"Why not?"

"There are complications," Tory said. "There's the house—"

"JoJo has wanted to rent that place for as long as I can remember."

"And what about my job?" Tory blurted.

"You're going to choose a job over the man who's just stolen your heart? If that's the case, you've completely lost it. Love always has to win. At least in my book. Timber Falls has a clinic and I happened to hear that they're expanding."

"You've got answers for everything, don't you? When did you become such a romantic?"

"When I see what's right in front of you, it's pretty easy."

Tory glanced at her suitcase. "I should stay."

"That's what I've been telling you."

She stood and dropped the lid down on her suitcase, because suddenly everything seemed clear. "I need to go find Griffin."

Griffin stared out at the mountains, white from all the snow they'd received over the past week, and tried to sort through his thoughts. He hadn't expected to fall in love. Hadn't expected someone like Tory to completely knock his world on end. Strange how it didn't seem to matter where he lived, as long as Tory was in his life. He wanted to buy a large plot of land and build a house, have a family and grow old right here in the middle of these mountains.

With her.

And that was the problem.

He couldn't expect her to leave everything for him. But maybe where he lived didn't matter. What mattered was who he was with.

Except she was gone and he'd missed his chance to stop her.

His phone rang and he pulled it out of his pocket to check the caller ID. It was Special Agent Mark Hill with the FBI. He hesitated then took the call.

"Deputy O'Callaghan," the man said once he'd answered. "We've got some good news for you."

Griffin stared out over the valley. "I could use a bit of good news right about now."

"We just arrested two more of Jinx's men and have been able to get statements from several of them. We'll still need Tory to testify, but with her, we have enough evidence, including the crimes that they've committed over the past few days, to send him and the majority of his organization away for the rest of their lives."

Griffin let out a long sigh of relief. "That's great news. I appreciate your taking the time to let me know."

"There's one other thing, as well. We caught the leak in our department. Evidence proves that Agent Parks disclosed classified information to Jinx for a hefty payout. He'll be facing prison time, as well."

"Wow. I'm glad to hear that."

"Would you mind passing on the news to Tory? I have a feeling that I'm the last one she wants to hear from at this point, even if it is good news."

"Of course, I'll tell her. And I know this is going to help her heal and move on."

He just wasn't sure he was ready for her to move on without him.

That was crazy. She had her own life and he had his. He should never have let the lines of duty and heart cross. He shifted his attention for a moment as a vehicle pulled into the gravel parking lot behind him and felt his heart race at the familiar rental car.

"Listen, Agent Hill, let me know if there's anything else you need from me. I need to go."

"Of course. If we have any questions, we'll give you a ring."

Griffin ended the call and put his hands in his pockets as Tory got out of the car and started toward him.

"Hey…" he said. "I'm surprised to see you."

"I was told I might find you here. It's beautiful up here."

"I know. I love it. It's a place I come when I need

some time to think." He hated the awkwardness that had developed between them. "I'd wanted to bring you here, actually. From up here you can see just how decked out the town is for Christmas, especially at night with all the lights."

"I can see why you love it."

"This weekend is a pre-Christmas festival where the season really gets kicked off. There's a parade where all of the riders wear costumes, sleigh rides, the tree lighting at city hall, music and food…" He was rambling and he had no idea why. Except that he hadn't expected to see her again and now that she was there, he didn't know what to say. "I was hoping you'd be here to see it, but more than that, I was afraid you might have left without saying goodbye."

Tory shook her head. "I couldn't do that."

"Good, because…" He hesitated.

Why did telling her how he was feeling right now seem harder than facing Jinx and his men?

"I'm going to miss you," he said. *And I still don't want you to go.*

"Can we talk for a few minutes?" she asked. *I've got the rest of my life for you.*

"Of course." He sat on the wooden bench and scooted to the side so she could sit next to him.

She shifted her attention from the valley below to him. "I was talking to my little sister—who I'm realizing isn't so little anymore—but anyway, she got me thinking about a few things."

Griffin felt his heart hammering in his chest, but waited for her to continue at her own pace.

He tried to brace himself for whatever she was about

to say, but the truth was, there was nothing she could say at the moment that could be worse than her leaving. Eventually his feelings would fade and life would go on.

Unless you're going to tell me you've decided to stay.

He shoved back the thought.

"I've told you some about my past," she said. "I lost my parents when I was twenty-one and ended up raising my little sister on my own. Now that my memory is back, intact for the most part, it's made me look at life differently. One of the reasons I came forward to testify against Jinx was to keep Elizabeth safe. I was afraid he'd come after her if he ever found out the truth. I've lost too many people I loved. I couldn't lose her." She let out a sharp breath. "That was why the only way I decided I could testify was to make a deal with the FBI. And you know what's crazy? Even when I couldn't remember my name, I still had that fear of losing those around me."

"I think that makes sense," he said. "I know what it's like to lose someone you care about. It changes you. Makes you more cautious while at the same time it makes you realize what's really important in life."

Griffin wasn't sure where she was going with the conversation, but he also didn't want to push her.

She fiddled with the end of her scarf. "Elizabeth told me this morning that she's accepted a job offer and is moving to Minneapolis in a couple of weeks."

"Wow…sounds like good news for her, but it has to be hard on you."

"I'm going to miss her, but she seems so excited. And I'm excited for her. She's a grown woman now, and I think it's the right thing to do."

"And you? How are you about letting her go?"

"It's going to be hard, but she reminded me that I need to have my own life. And I'm not sure that's something I've had for a long time. I need to let her go. Need to figure out what I want to do." Tory looked up and caught his gaze. "I'm thinking about staying here."

"Wait a minute…here in Timber Falls?"

He had to be missing something, but he couldn't jump to conclusions.

"I love it here, but the town isn't the only reason I want to stay." She laced her fingers around her knee and stared out across the valley. "You see, I met someone, and I think no matter how much my head tells me to run, if I listen to my heart, it's telling me to stay. Stay and find out what could happen between us."

"What are you saying?"

"I'm thinking about taking a job in Timber Falls at the clinic."

He felt his heart stop at the admission. "And you're sure about this?"

"My sister reminded me of a few things this morning, but honestly, I don't think I've ever been so sure of anything in my whole life. I just needed someone to push me in the right direction."

Griffin couldn't help but match her smile. "So you really think you might stick around? Because I know this girl I met not too long ago. She's changed how I look at life and made me realize that it doesn't matter where I am as long as I'm with someone I love."

Tory scooted a couple inches toward him. "If the offer's still available, I'm ready to take a chance on love. To take a chance on you."

He pulled her to him then brushed his lips across hers. "Then maybe it's time I ask you out on an official date."

She pulled away and laughed. "Wait a minute. I never kiss a guy on a first date, let alone before a first date."

"Okay." He kissed her again. "Then we need to simply skip ahead at least a dozen dates—maybe two—in our relationship, because what we've been through over the past couple of weeks has to count for something."

"True." Her grin broadened. "That means I suppose I could make an exception."

He tilted up her chin with his thumb and caught her gaze. "You are the exception, Tory. Do you understand that? You waltzed into my life and have affected me in a way no one else ever has. I knew I was looking for something, I just didn't know what. But now I know I love you and don't want this—us—to end."

She smiled back at him. "I love you, too, and I've realized something about finding fulfillment. It really doesn't have anything to do with where you are, but rather who you are with."

"Exactly." He put his arms around her and pulled her against him before kissing her again. "And you're the one I want to be with."

* * * * *

If you enjoyed this story by Lisa Harris,
pick up these other thrilling titles:

Taken
Desperate Escape
Desert Secrets
Fatal Cover-Up
Deadly Exchange
No Place to Hide
Sheltered by the Soldier

Available now from Love Inspired Suspense!

Find more great reads at www.LoveInspired.com

Dear Reader,

Thank you so much for letting me share Tory and Griffin's story with you! I loved the chance to explore the lives of another O'Callaghan brother. I'm sure you can agree that there's always something extra special about the Christmas season, as it's a time for family, gratitude and hope. Especially in a place as beautiful as Colorado.

Like in the story, though, life also has its darker moment. Moments when you feel overwhelmed with what's going on around you. Maybe that's where you are right now, feeling as if you can't go on. Remember to keep your eyes on Him, because you are not alone. When you go through the deep waters, He will be with you.

Watch for more page-turning suspense in the next book in the series from Timber Falls with Caden O'Callaghan!

Lisa Harris

WE HOPE YOU ENJOYED THIS BOOK!

Love Inspired® SUSPENSE

Uncover the truth in these thrilling
stories of faith in the face of crime
from Love Inspired Suspense.
Discover six new books available
every month, wherever books
are sold!

LoveInspired.com

AVAILABLE THIS MONTH FROM
Love Inspired® Suspense

TRUE BLUE K-9 UNIT CHRISTMAS
True Blue K-9 Unit • by Laura Scott and Maggie K. Black

The holidays bring danger and love in these two brand-new novellas, where a K-9 officer teams up with a paramedic to find her ex's killer before she and her daughter become the next victims, and an officer and his furry partner protect a tech whiz someone wants silenced.

AMISH CHRISTMAS HIDEAWAY
by Lenora Worth

Afraid for her life after witnessing a double homicide, Alisha Braxton calls the one person she knows can help her—private investigator Nathan Craig. Now hiding in Amish country, can they stay one step ahead of a murderer who's determined she won't survive Christmas?

HOLIDAY HOMECOMING SECRETS
by Lynette Eason

After their friend is killed, detective Jade Hollis and former soldier Bryce Kingsley join forces to solve the case. But searching for answers proves deadly—and Jade's hiding a secret. Can she live long enough to give Bryce a chance to be a father to the daughter he never knew existed?

CHRISTMAS WITNESS PURSUIT
by Lisa Harris

When an ambush leaves two FBI agents dead and her memory wiped, the only person witness Tory Faraday trusts is the sheriff's deputy who saved her. But even hiding on Griffin O'Callaghan's family ranch isn't quite safe enough after a dangerous criminal escapes from custody with one goal: finding her.

SILENT NIGHT SUSPECT
by Sharee Stover

Framed for the murder of a cartel boss, Asia Stratton must clear her name... before she ends up dead or in jail. State trooper Slade Jackson's convinced the crime is tied to the police corruption Asia's late husband—and his former partner—suspected. But can they prove it?

FATAL FLASHBACK
by Kellie VanHorn

Attacked and left for dead, all Ashley Thompson remembers is her name. But after park ranger Logan Everett rescues her, she discovers she's an undercover FBI agent searching for a mole in the rangers. Without blowing her cover, can she convince Logan to help her expose the traitor...before the investigation turns fatal?

LISATMBPA1219

SPECIAL EXCERPT FROM

Love Inspired.
SUSPENSE

*Danger has caught up with Ashley Willis, and she'll
have to trust the local deputy in order to stay one step
ahead of a killer who wants her dead.*

Read on for a sneak preview of
Secret Mountain Hideout *by Terri Reed,*
available January 2020 from Love Inspired Suspense.

It couldn't be.

Ice filled Ashley Willis's veins despite the spring
sunshine streaming through the living room windows of
the Bristle Township home in Colorado where she rented
a bedroom.

Disbelief cemented her feet to the floor, her gaze
riveted to the horrific images on the television screen.

Flames shot out of the two-story building she'd hoped
never to see again. Its once bright red awnings were now
singed black and the magnificent stained glass windows
depicting the image of an angry bull were no more.

She knew that place intimately.

The same place that haunted her nightmares.

The newscaster's words assaulted her. She grabbed on
to the back of the faded floral couch for support.

"In a fiery inferno, the posh Burbank restaurant The
Matador was consumed by a raging fire in the wee hours
of the morning. Firefighters are working diligently to
douse the flames. So far there have been no fatalities.
However, there has been one critical injury."

LISEXP1219R

Ashley's heart thumped painfully in her chest, reminding her to breathe. Concern for her friend Gregor, the man who had safely spirited her away from the Los Angeles area one frightening night a year and a half ago when she'd witnessed her boss, Maksim Sokolov, kill a man, thrummed through her. She had to know what happened. She had to know if Gregor was the one injured.

She had to know if this had anything to do with her.

"Mrs. Marsh," Ashley called out. "Would you mind if I use your cell phone?"

Her landlady, a widow in her mideighties, appeared in the archway between the living room and kitchen. Her hot-pink tracksuit hung on her stooped shoulders, but it was her bright smile that always tugged at Ashley's heart. The woman was a spitfire, with her blue-gray hair and her kind green eyes behind thick spectacles.

"Of course, dear. It's in my purse." She pointed to the black satchel on the dining room table. "Though you know, as I keep saying, you should get your own cell phone. It's not safe for a young lady to be walking around without any means of calling for help."

They had been over this ground before. Ashley didn't want anything attached to her name.

Or rather, her assumed identity—Jane Thompson.

Don't miss
Secret Mountain Hideout *by Terri Reed,*
available January 2020 wherever
Love Inspired Suspense books and ebooks are sold.

LoveInspired.com

Get 4 FREE REWARDS!

We'll send you 2 FREE Books
plus 2 FREE Mystery Gifts.

85'60

Love Inspired® Suspense books feature Christian characters facing challenges to their faith... and lives.

FREE Value Over $20